Shaping Our Global Future

POSTCARDS FROM SCOTLAND

Series editor: Carol Craig

Advisory group:
Fred Shedden, Chair, Centre for Confidence
and Well-being;
Professor Phil Hanlon;
Jean Urquhart MSP

Shaping Our Global Future

A guide for young people

Derek Brown

ARGYLL ✠ PUBLISHING

First published by Argyll Publishing an imprint of Capercaillie Books in 2015.

Registered Office 1 Rutland Court, Edinburgh

A catalogue record of this book is available from the British Library

ISBN 978-1-908931-77-1

Printed by Bell & Bain Ltd, Glasgow

Contents

Contents

Acknowledgements

Thanks to Lesley Stopani, Susan Wilson and Pete Booth for their moral support and concern to inform young people about global issues. Some of these young people were pupils of Oldmachar Academy – an inspirational audience for early versions of this material. I am proud them.

As the work developed, senior educationalists in the BOSCH group read various versions and gave advice. They include Eddie Broadley, Dr Jim Scott, Gerry Lyons, Dave McClure and Ben Davis. This book owes much to the crucible of BOCSH debates and so I thank the whole group.

Cathy Begley, Alistair Wilson, Henry Hepburn, Craig Munro, Rebecca Wallace and Douglas Brown offered helpful support. Further back in time, work with Stuart Heron, Gerry Sludden and Dr Paul Thomson on the Inspiring Enquiring Minds programme informed this book. The learning we did was not wasted gentlemen. And even further back, Simon Murray introduced me to the world of IB Theory of Knowledge, for which I am most thankful.

For their continued belief, I must thank Dr Alan Britton, whose vision of education for the future is unique in Scotland, and also Carol Craig, who provided me with advice and support. I also thank the wonderful Rebecca Alexander and wee Magnus Brown.

Lastly, I thank my son Euan Brown for his genuine interest in global issues and his selfless support for a project devoted to his younger sister. Effective altruism in practice!

This book would not have been as it is without these great people.

Derek Brown, 2015

Preface

Dear Daughter

I guess that as daughters grow up, fathers become more aware of their own age. Worrying about the future is also part of the process of watching your children become adults. As I write this it is late 2014 and I have been pondering the future that you, your children and grandchildren will have.

You are sixteen years old and the 21st century will unfold in your lifetime. If your great grand-daughter is born in 2084, she will turn sixteen in 2100. At that point, I would be 130 years old. I'm sure I won't still be around and I can say with certainty that I have no desire to be. But I am concerned about what the world will be like for your great grand-daughter's generation.

When it comes to your sixteenth birthday present, I suppose a book about your personal and global future might not have been the most obvious thing for me to give you. But here it is. I hope you like it.

I try to balance sources of hope about the future with some of the issues human beings will have to tackle in order to thrive. I consider some incredible global wonders human beings have created and some particular global challenges people your age will face in their lifetime.

The twenty-second century is starting to take shape in our imaginations. It leaks into our lives in strange ways. We can imagine new technologies we are likely to use and increasingly intuitive ways we will employ them. Tele-communication devices have almost become part of our identities in the last couple of decades. But it might also be a century in which we will need more resources like food, water and energy to provide for a much larger human population. So we are going to have to think seriously about sharing resources.

In describing some of the challenges your generation will face, I emphasise opportunities people might have and the conditions in which they might live.

In attempting to establish what the actual state of our human species is currently, I try to avoid scaremongering, but have to acknowledge that there are serious problems ahead, and make suggestions on how these can be tackled.

You could look at this book as a kind of map of global issues. It is written from the perspective of someone who is generally interested in them. I balance differing views, especially where experts disagree. One of the exciting parts about writing about events that have not happened is that you sometimes need to speculate. I have done that at key moments and suggested possible scenarios that might affect you.

---

[1]   Reference material can be accessed at
      http://www.postcardsfromscotland.co.uk/book_08.html

I have avoided writing in too academic a manner. I provide reference points which best fit the way you might research things for yourself. So, I refer to on-line sources you can research quickly and without cost. I use easy to find material from sources you will be familiar with. In the e-book edition, these sources are included as hyperlinks. They are omitted from the print version but can be accessed on line. At other times I refer to or recommend books.

I am writing in Aberdeen, during a dark winter. This book has an international focus. Hugh MacDiarmid, the early twentieth century Scottish poet, suggested that a Scottish moment could be a universal moment. I hope that this book is such a moment. In it we journey from China to Africa. From Ancient Rome to Canada. From outer space to Glasgow.

This is a wee book about your human future. It is a father's gift. An act of hope.

Lots of love
Dad

Introduction

We live our lives in the present. Every day we go about our normal routines. We eat, drink and sleep to fulfil our most basic needs. We are social beings, so we make and lose friendships throughout our lives. We dedicate ourselves to people, things or ideas in which we find pleasure or meaning. We love and we hate. We hold grudges and forgive. We get ill and get better. We make money to live financially. At times, we ponder death. We have moments of great happiness and other times where sadness overwhelms us. We search for sense, or meaning in ourselves through experience. Such things go into what we know life to be.

We live our lives in the present, but the past and future interrupt the here and now.

Things that have happened to us linger. Sometimes, we convince ourselves that we can't do things because of past problems and become overwhelmed. At other times, we confront past mistakes and learn from them, gathering experience and using it to help us be better or stronger the next time. The memory of people and things which have hurt us can haunt us. But friendships have a power to transform us and we can take pleasure from mementos of the past.

And the future too leaks into our present lives in strange ways. We drift off for a moment and find ourselves wondering about the lives we might lead, places we might go, things we might do. And then come some wider questions about the world that we and our children (and indeed their children) will inhabit. And, when we think about these things, we experience the same mixture of hope and dread that affects our daily personal lives.

We live our lives in the present, but increasingly, the future is a source of anxiety.

How we live our individual lives will affect our personal futures. How human beings as a whole species live will affect all our futures. People have learned to recycle waste because they think it is a good thing to do – 'thinking globally, acting locally' as the soundbite urges.

People plan careers based on their best guess about what the future will be like, especially the economy. So when they plan to go into certain industries like oil and gas, the media, or the health service, they are in part assuming there will be a need for such work in future.

In democracies, people vote for parties or leaders that present the most compelling picture of the future – the economy is a major concern. The party which convinces people they will create jobs and wealth often wins the trust of voters.

We live our lives in the present, but the present gets faster and faster.

The unpredictability of the future can lead us to take comfort in the present. We block out things like global warming until the next news story about tornadoes. We eat foods without thinking until the next public health scare. Even friendships we form are subject to change. We invest lots of time in people we like, only for them to move to new places and change how they see themselves, making us think about whether we still like them. Technological revolutions happen faster and faster.

The future nags at us, haunting our imaginations, with uncertainty about what might happen. What will happen to us when we are older? What will our children experience? Will my job be safe? What if I get ill? What kind of person do I want to be? What will others think of me?

Some of these questions are personal and some relate to things we can't control. Elements of our global future leak into our personal concerns.

The future is coming and it could be very challenging. It may be the best of human times. Alternatively, it could well end up being the worst.

The worst of all possible worlds – and the best as well

Let's imagine the worst for a moment. It's the year 2100. There is no human life on earth. Humans have brought about their own destruction and our race been exterminated. Earth is a wasted planet, with minimal life – trillions of lives have evaporated from all species.

This might seem like a very gloomy picture straight from science fiction but researchers at Oxford University recently published an academic study about the future. The study, led by Professor Nick Bostrom, looked at how likely it was that human beings would survive as a species until 2100. They looked at (existential) threats to human survival such as war, terrorism, disease, overpopulation, lack of food and water, et cetera.

Bostrom came up with a worrying statistic. According to him, there is roughly a 20 per cent chance that humanity will not survive till 2100. That is a four to one chance. If you were a betting person and you waged £50 on that happening, you'd make £200 on the bet. It's just that you wouldn't be around to collect the money – and there wouldn't be much to spend it on.

2100 is only 85 years away. It's not a long time – the entire adult life and more of a 16 year old who is reading this. If researchers are right, there is a fairly good chance humans will do things that could destroy all of us in our lifetimes.

On the bright side, there is an 80 per cent chance we will survive – though survival may involve compromising on some things we currently take for granted: food, fresh water, freedoms, and clean air, to name a few.

There are some reasons for optimism. For example, the fact that humanity has progressed to the point it has; the amazing scientific and technological advances of the past few hundred years; increased international collaboration and trust between countries, especially to achieve global targets like the Millennium Development Goals; and our greater awareness of the things that could destroy us and their power to do so.

So, given all this, I am posing a few questions:

- What will it mean to be human in 2100?
- How might human beings live good lives in the future?

- How can we make sure humanity does not destroy itself in the process of evolving from where we are now, to where we might be?
- What kind of learning do we need to do as a species to evolve further and survive?
- And finally, to what extent should we feel optimistic about our future?

Global wonders and global challenges

The Seven Wonders of the Ancient World celebrated great achievements of human culture – particular buildings, statues or gardens that were amazing to see around the time historians typically refer to as the ancient Greek period (preceding the Christian period).

The people who compiled the list of ancient wonders may not have known about the Great Wall of China (sometimes called the eighth wonder), or the cultural achievements in South America. The list focused on Persia, North Africa, Turkey and Greece – the most prominent civilizations of the period. The wonders were the:

- Great Pyramid at Giza
- Hanging Gardens at Babylon
- Temple of Artemis at Ephesus
- Statue of Zeus at Olympia
- Mausoleum at Halicarnassus
- Colossus at Rhodes
- Lighthouse of Alexandria

The Great Pyramid is the only one still standing – the most ancient of them all.

You may wonder why people bothered compiling such lists. Perhaps they wanted to inspire others, or celebrate certain remarkable cultures. As humans progressed over centuries, their achievements became more diverse and inspiring. I provide a list of seven modern global wonders in what follows.

Global challenges are easier to define, because we can draw on a great deal of available research and publically held information. You could try coming up with your own lists – and reasons why you would include, or exclude, things.

The most important thing, for me, is that we should all be thinking more seriously about this. Future studies is not a subject typically taught at school, it is something we have to do for ourselves. And since the things that affect our future seem to be subject to constant change, we need a map.

So here goes . . .

Seven modern global wonders

The Seven Wonders of the Ancient World were symbols of the highest culture, beauty or achievement of the period. But what are their modern equivalents?

The ones I have chosen represent important human achievements. Some are physical constructions, others are documents and some are technologies. Each highlights a powerful source of optimism. I used four criteria. For me it was important that:

- The wonder is a major human achievement
- Its existence shows humans capability to transform themselves
- Significant learning had to be done by people to make it happen

- Its existence could be part of the solution to the challenges facing humanity.

The modern global wonders I have chosen to fit these four criteria are:

1 The International Space Station
2 Olympic Games
3 Genetic engineering
4 Telecommunications
5 CERN
6 Electronic gaming
7 The United Nations Declaration of the Rights of the Child.

I have emphasised science and technology, but there are cultural and political wonders as well. A question might be: what are your seven modern wonders?

It was tempting to include cinema – possibly, like the Great Wall of China in the ancient list, as the eighth wonder. In the end gaming edged in to the main list as it engages so many young people and is a source of learning. It came down to a choice between *Angry Birds* and *Avatar*, and I chose *Angry Birds*. When I was sixteen in 1986, the film *Aliens* would have out-done *Super Mario* as a recreational experience – even though games were increasingly interesting.

But the high-speed, permanent revolution of gaming has transformed the experiences it can provide, making it more seductive.

Seven current global challenges

In thinking about future challenges, I drew from various sources but have chosen issues which:

- Have the capacity to affect the human population on a massive scale
- Could be destructive to humanity
- Would require significant human learning to resolve them
- Would require huge collaborative effort by nations to address the challenge.

The list below shows modern global challenges that fit these criteria:

1 Global war
2 Terrorism
3 Disease (Pandemic)
4 Human population expansion
5 Lack of resource
6 Climate change
7 Gap between rich and poor

Of course, I've chosen these challenges in 2014 and they may look completely different in 2100. Chemical terrorism could be a much bigger threat. Global wars might be fought by remote artificial, or super intelligences (drones or superdrones). And, as scientists anticipate, some changes in the earth's climate may not be reversible.

We may also enter an era of super-rich and ultra-poor, even more so than now. And scarcity of basic resources (food, water and energy) might present a different kind of challenge from today.

Wonders and challenges have not been ranked in order. Some global challenges provide sources of hope and opportunity; some wonders contain some terrifying or problematic aspects. Nothing is simple. Analysis and understanding is required. I just ask some awkward questions in key places to encourage people to think critically about the future.

The International Space Station

My first global wonder is the International Space Station (ISS). NASA has posted films of it on YouTube in which astronauts, like Sunita Williams, show you around.

The amazing ability of humans to aspire and achieve is perhaps best shown by this structure orbiting the earth. It has been built through international cooperation, with countries working in shared interest. Five space agencies share responsibility for the project which is governed by treaties. Astronauts and cosmonauts from fifteen countries have visited it.

The space station is the size of a football stadium – over a hundred metres long, around 80 metres wide and 20 high. It has been operated by teams of astronauts and cosmonauts for over 13 years. It orbits earth in just over 90 minutes and travels at a speed of over 17,000 miles per hour to do that – over 250 miles above us in space. Just imagining this is mind boggling. Human beings are up there just now, living in space! And they come from all parts of the world.

ISS's goal is to further the project of human life and travel in space. It conducts experiments which add to human knowledge in physics, chemistry, biology and other disciplines. Most importantly, perhaps, is the knowledge that relates to how humans cope in the artificial environment of the station itself.

Canadian astronaut, Chris Hadfield, embodies this work. He led the space station and worked with astronauts and cosmonauts from different countries. He is the first Canadian in space, but inspires young people from countries around the world to imagine following in his footsteps.

Where does the impulse to explore and create come from?

Human beings like to set and achieve goals. In doing so we look forward positively to the future and think about what we want to accomplish. This is part of how we build our sense of self-worth and improve the circumstances we find ourselves in. Some historic examples show how goals have shaped human progress.

In AD 84 Roman soldiers travelled north towards the area west of Aberdeen, where I am sitting now, writing this book. They came to engage the Caledonian tribes in battle. Writer Kenneth White has written eloquently about how Roman soldiers must have seen the place as a savage, cold land at the very edge of existence. They called the territory Alba (from the Latin word for white) because of its white hills. (White's work on what he calls Geopoetics is about trying to find a kind of universal poetry in the world.)

The battle of Mons Graupius actually took place somewhere in the Grampian mountain range, west of Aberdeen. The Romans won, a historical moment that symbolises the quest to conquer the environment and other races – a factor in human development.

Almost a thousand years later, in 1000AD, a young Viking called Leif Erikson journeyed west past Scotland from Norway, aiming for land he hoped to find beyond Greenland, now known as Newfoundland. Many believe him the first European to set foot in the North American continent. His aim was not simply to explore but also to find riches. His journey was full of danger. As he negotiated the deep seas of the Arctic Circle, he did not know whether he would survive, let alone succeed.

Go forward another thousand years. Imagine a young woman, Amelia Earhart, preparing to take off in an aeroplane in 1932 from the same area of Newfoundland. She was attempting to be the first woman aviator to cross the Atlantic in a solo flight. Her journey took her back the way Viking explorers came a millennium before. She landed fourteen hours later in a field in Northern Ireland, not far from where Erikson once set sail – 300 miles from where Agricola battled Caledonians.

These three events, each roughly 1000 years apart, show the human narrative of discovery and development – endless questing for new ideas and territories. Whether you are talking about the years of the Roman campaign in Caledonia, Leif Erikson's voyage west of several months, or Amelia Earhart's fourteen hour flight east, or the hurtling orbit of the International Space Station, setting and achieving goals is part of who we are.

As human beings have advanced, science, technology and discovery have all been at the heart of that advancement –

from Roman weaponry, to Viking longboats, to Earhart's bright red Lockheed Vega 5B aeroplane. And latest in line, the space station.

A 'space odyssey'

Aspiration to explore space is a symbol of our natural curiosity and spirit of adventure. Chris Hadfield says:

> For thousands of years, people sailed in rivers and up and down the coast. And only after they had invented so many things – navigation, food supply, really good sails, ships they could count on – did they turn away from shore and go over the horizon. They had to invent a lot of things first. There may have been people that went over the horizon, but they probably didn't come back, because they didn't know enough stuff yet. And we are, right now, sailing within the sight of shore. We're trying to figure out all those things as we go around the world, so that when you do fire your engines and go 40 percent faster and leave the Earth, and it's been really hard to turn around and come back, that you can count on your sailing ship, that it's going to keep you alive and get you where you want to go. And that's what the Space Station is. It is the crucible where we're learning and testing and figuring out all those things so that we can go further, which is inevitably what we're going to do.

In 2008 I co-led a government funded project in Glasgow devoted to informing young people about global issues. We staged conferences for young people from around Scotland. Chris Hadfield, and a number of astronauts and cosmonauts, attended one conference and spoke to student delegates.

The astronauts and cosmonauts talked eloquently about the human dimension of the space station project; in particular the spirit of international cooperation that grew between them. They talked about how being together in space, surveying earth from above, broke barriers between nations and raised awareness of their shared humanity. This was a powerful testimony of the project's potential, especially given the relationship between the countries involved. There had been times when they seemed close to war.

Space and war and peace

In the 1950s and 1960s, as the Cold War between the USA and USSR took hold, people on both sides of what used to be called 'the iron curtain' saw space exploration as a race to be won. Each side tried to show how powerful and technologically advanced it was. Partly it was about the different political systems of democracy and communism competing for dominance. The USSR had the first space flight; the USA landed the first man on the moon.

In 1975, the first meeting in space between Russian cosmonauts and United States astronauts took place; a historic moment. Half a century later, it is both a source of hope and a sign of progress that space exploration is a collaborative effort – not an arms race between nations on the brink of war.

So let's hope that international projects built on collaboration and mutual interest can be a way forward – progressively breaking down barriers and building trust between people and nations. If countries can collaborate so effectively on a space project, what might happen if we focused our collective energy on conserving humanity and our planet?

If the astronauts' human bond can be replicated on earth, perhaps there is hope. We might learn to take more of a world view in the planning of human societies and in the way we live our individual lives.

Professor Steven Hawking draws a different conclusion from the lessons learned in space exploration, 'I believe that the long term future of humans is in space . . . It will be difficult to avoid disaster on planet earth in the next hundred years, let alone the next thousand or million. The human race shouldn't have all of its eggs in one basket, or on one planet.'

From one viewpoint, Hawking may be simply endorsing a kind of scientific optimism that many, including Chris Hadfield, would share. On the other hand, he expresses a deep pessimism about our capacity to surive on earth. Others might take the view that humans should learn to conserve this planet and find more effective ways to treat its resources.

Human creativity

There have been technological by-products of space exploration as well. NASA claims hundreds of technologies we use every day are spin offs from space research. These include things like water purifiers, prosthetic limbs and baby food formula.

This illustrates an important point – scientific by-products can be really useful, even if scientists don't always achieve their stated goals.

Humans have been inventors and creators at every stage of history. With progress, we've reflected what it means to be human. We have built complex systems of government. We have created beauty in art and literature. In recent times we've learned to travel in space.

Underpinning these achievements has been the fundamental human desire to look over the horizon and imagine what might be there. Deeper still, possibly, is the desire for a better way to live.

The problem can be that the process of developing science and exploration (as is the case with the ISS) can sometimes seem at odds with sustainable ways of living, especially when it is wrapped up with the commercial interests of powerful nations and wealthy corporations. In that spirit, our first wonder has a problematic dimension that needs to be acknowledged.

Most inspiring, though, is the idea of astronauts and cosmonauts, from nations not long ago embroiled in cold war conflict which threatened human existence, up there, right now in space, collaborating and sharing a deeper human concern for us all. If we could replicate and share this human bond more widely, our future would be more secure.

We might do well to reflect on the following questions:

1　How can we share the positive messages of international collaboration on such projects as the International Space Station?
2　How can lessons from this project be translated into other projects?
3　Should we be optimistic or pessimistic about the potential of science to solve global challenges?

Global War

Think about what happens in relationships when people fall out: name calling, bullying, even violence. Communities partly define themselves by how they differ from other groups. Differences become sources of tension. As individuals we make friends with some people and not others. Some people get discounted and excluded from groups. Other groups might not like our friends and might mock us. We retaliate, and so on . . .

Belonging to a particular group, a local community, or even a country can be an important element in helping us define who we are – helping our sense of belonging. But situations can arise where the existence of one group becomes a problem for another group (perhaps one feels threatened, or sees they will have greater power if they cannot subjugate another group).

Sometimes nation states band together with others to act as allies in furthering their mutual interest. This can protect them and afford a greater chance of success. Sometimes a nation can become powerful through war. In World War II, a group of countries came together to stop Nazi Germany becoming dominant.

Human relations on an international level reflect those that can exist between individuals and smaller communities. Differences become exaggerated and trust breaks down. Having greater awareness of global citizenship might encourage people to find ways to coexist with people of different views and cultures. Living peacefully with others could be a key issue in the twenty-second century, as it is in certain parts of the world today.

Nation states: status and sources of conflict

Countries which have experienced peace for generations can forget how destructive war can be. Even if your country has taken part in an armed conflict abroad, you may grow up never having been touched personally by war. Many people nowadays only experience war through media images. But personal experience of war can be devastating.

There are over two hundred recognised countries in the world, 193 of which are current members of the United Nations (UN). Sixteen of them have 'disputed status'. This means at least one other country believes it should not be allowed to exist. People have gone to war throughout history over the very idea of nationhood and identity and continue to do so, as the struggle of the Kurdish people in Turkey, Syria and Iraq shows.

Israel, for example, is not recognized by over thirty countries. It has been periodically engaged in conflict with Palestinian territories on its borders. Palestinian groups do not recognise Israel as a country and Israel does not recognise Palestine. Each side accuses the other of acts of terrorism and war crimes. The conflict has taken innumerable lives.

The USA won independence from Britain in 1760. When some southern states tried to withdraw from the union in 1860, a civil war ensued for four years. During the war, each side had its own government – the Confederacy government sat in Richmond for most of the civil war whilst the Union's capital remained in Washington DC. So the nationhood of the most powerful country was in doubt just 150 years ago. An estimated 750,000 people died in the conflict.

There are around a dozen global conflicts right now that lead to over 1000 deaths per conflict each year. There are also protests against how countries are governed which also claim large numbers of lives. The nature and identity of nations can lead to acts of war within and between countries, as well as between groups of people seeking national status.

Global war and human progress

When you watch the news, you often see images of people suffering from war. But Steven Pinker, distinguished psychologist and scholar, argues in a recent book *The Better Angels of our Nature* (2011) that violence in human societies has declined with time. Indeed in a TED talk on the subject he argues we 'are probably living in the most peaceful time in the history of our species.'

Pinker charts the development of human violence over time, looking at how the likelihood of being murdered has vastly reduced for human beings over the past 10,000 years. His statistics also show 'from 1950 there has been a steep decline in numbers of deaths per conflict per year. The death rate goes down from 65000 deaths per conflict per year in 1950 to 2000 in this decade, as horrific as it is.'

He thinks modern communications make us more aware of the effects of war and increases our disapproval of it. He puts the warring tendency of humans down to a deep instinct to attack others in order to protect what we ourselves have. War has undoubtedly helped technological development – before the civil war the USA was mainly agricultural, and through war became industrialised. It is an irony that at times war has helped human progress.

The tension: science and citizenship

The architect of the International Day of Peace, Jeremy Gilley, was motivated by the human cost of the USA's use of nuclear weapons against Japan in World War II. In his TED talk he tells us:

> My grandfather was a prisoner of war. He saw the bomb go off at Nagasaki. It poisoned his blood. He died when I was eleven. He was my hero. 700 men left, 23 men came back. Two died on the boat and 21 hit the ground.

For over fifty years, with access to weapons of mass destruction, humanity has had the power to wipe itself out. Some countries possess nuclear weapons as a deterrent – to stop others attacking them. Generations will be burdened by the fact such weapons exist whilst continuing to ensure no one uses them. From one viewpoint, these weapons are a technological marvel; from another, they are terrifying.

Decades ago philosopher Bertrand Russell asserted: 'To improve the fighting quality of separate states without having the means of preventing war is a road to universal destruction.' Humanity has arrived at an important historic point: we can destroy ourselves through weapons of huge technological power and precision. But we only need these due to the ways in which nations and peoples interact. This is one example of the complex relationship that exists between science and citizenship.

Child soldiers

In a warzone, everyone is affected and children's lives are often destroyed as a consequence. But in some places, even today, children are involved in warfare as soldiers. Some are seasoned soldiers who have not only seen death but also torture and rape.

Peace Direct estimates 300,000 children world-wide are soldiers, 40 per cent of whom are girls:

> Children are more easily manipulated than adult fighters. Many children will fight on the frontlines . . . Girls are often forced into sexual slavery. Many are recruited by force – stolen from their families and forced to fight. In some cases children are made to kill their relatives so they can never return home.

Sierra Leone emerged from a brutal civil war with international support, including a peace keeping force, which was deployed to disarm militia groups. A UN report from 2000 quotes a teenage girl from Sierra Leone: 'I've seen people get their hands cut off, a ten-year old girl raped and then die, and so many men and women burned alive . . . So many times I just cried inside my heart because I didn't dare cry out loud.' She had been abducted by an armed group.

There are particular concerns about groups in Rwanda who use child soldiers. A press release from Child Soldiers International (2013) stated:

Since June 2012, reports from UN and non-governmental organisations (NGOs) have consistently pointed to the role of Rwandan officials in supporting the M23. This has included assistance in recruitment – in Rwanda's territory – of Rwandan and Congolese children to be deployed in hostilities in the DRC. The M23 is listed in the annex of the last UN Secretary-General's report as a party that recruits and uses children.

Consequences for children in wars are horrific. On the internet you can find many clips which show the plight of children fighting for armed groups.

Peace building: the idea and the practice

'Peace building' studies shows the importance of learning across subject disciplines. According to the Oxford University Peace Studies Network:

The concept of 'peacebuilding' has come to be central to peace studies. Successful outcomes in peacebuilding depend on inclusive perspectives. The study of peace [draws] on politics and international relations, economics, development; gender, media, environmental studies; history; war and conflict studies; education, anthropology, law, ethics and theology to name only a few.

In 1795 in a short essay called 'Perpetual peace' philosopher Immanuel Kant wrote about how nations should live in peace. He argues countries should be considered similarly to people – with rights. He asserts 'No state shall by force interfere with the constitution or government of another state.' He also writes: 'No state shall, during war, permit such acts of hostility which would make mutual confidence in the subsequent peace impossible: such are the employment of assassins, poisoners, breach of capitulation, and incitement to treason in the opposing state.'

Kant sought a moral code for war similar to the one used to protect people from crime. Some may find this idealistic, but it does underpin Geneva Conventions and the work of the United Nations. By Kant's rationale, UK and USA should not have intervened in Iraq in 2003, for example.

Peacebuilding is therefore an academic discipline but the term also refers to practical activities. In conflict affected areas around the world, peace organisations devote themselves to building up relationships between groups. This involves courageous work, tackling attitudes and challenging views that might lead to acts of violence or war.

Peace Direct reports:

> In the turbulent mountain region between Pakistan and Afghanistan, a 23-year-old peace builder has founded a network of peace activists – a brave band of young people whose mission is to halt the spread of religious extremism and rescue their peers from recruitment into militant organisations.

This story of a young woman, Gulalai Ismael, building peace around her speaks of a courage we admire in other humans but rightly leads us to wonder if we would be able to show such courage ourselves, if we were in similar circumstances.

The future

The International Day of Peace is commemorated on the 21st of September. It came about as the result of Jeremy Gilley's activism, 'There was no starting point for peace. There was no day when humanity came together. And if we united and inter-culturally cooperated then that might shift the level of consciousness around the fundamental issues humanity faces.'

In 2008, on the first International Day of Peace, there was a 70 per cent reduction in violence in Afghanistan, as both sides respected the day.

There is clearly hope, expressed by Steven Pinker, Jeremy Gilley and Gulalai Ismael. But how we deal with conflict between people may be crucial to the kind of human future we have. In the world our children and grandchildren will inhabit, hanging on to a sense of shared humanity that balances national interests with people's basic right to live in peace may well be crucial to human survival, or at least to ways large groups of the human population are able to live their lives.

Some questions for us might be:

1 How can we promote peace through our individual actions?
2 How can we encourage governments to act in the interests of peace?
3 How are we to deal with groups or nations who threaten peace?

WONDER 2

The Olympic and Paralympic Games and What They Mean

In 2012 the Olympic Games in London celebrated the coming together of nations in sporting competition. The scale and reach of the games is one of the reasons I think it qualifies as a global wonder. The Olympic Organisation's website claims there were athletes from 204 Olympic Committees (nations of the world) and over 10,000 athletes. There were almost nine million attendees who bought tickets for events and there were an estimated four billion worldwide spectators. 200,000 people were employed to staff the games. The Olympic Village served 45,000 meals per day.

Contests were hard fought and athletes pushed themselves to feats of incredible dexterity, skill, speed and endurance. The London Games recorded thirty-two world records in eight different sports. It was an event of great scale and achievement.

Academic, Maurice Roche, defines the Olympics as one of a number of mega events: 'large-scale cultural (including commercial and sporting) events, which have a dramatic character, mass popular appeal and international significance.'

The five interlocking Olympic rings, (the Games emblem) symbolise the interconnectedness of the five continents and show their universalism.

The Olympic ideal

The Olympic Organisation cites a number of important ideals – the most famously quoted is: 'It is not only about winning, but mainly about participating, making progress against personal goals, striving to be and to do our best in our daily lives and benefiting from the combination of a strong body, will and mind.'

Behind the games lies a deeper set of ideas about celebrating the underlying humanity we share. Through the Games we see the power of global citizenship to forge friendships across boundaries of race, class, gender and physical ability.

The Olympic ethos helps us feel part of something that takes us out of ourselves. It allows us to feel pride in our own nation, but also increases our understanding and respect for peoples from other parts of the world. Through competition we come to respect achievements of people about whom we might have had preconceptions. The Olympic ideal is for people to compete on an equal footing: men and women; people of all colours and capacities; of all sexualities.

In describing aspirations of the Youth Olympic Games, International Olympic Committee President, Jacques Rogge said, 'Our hope is if young people can learn to respect each other on the field of play, they may transfer this to other parts of their daily lives.'

Human being and identity

The idea of respect assumes a standard of behaviour we might expect of ourselves and others. Arguably, everyone has different standards, but the fact we have an agreed statement of human rights shows that, across the world, we broadly agree about how people should be treated.

The awareness you have of yourself is partly defined by relationships with others. In early childhood, your actions are guided by the ideas of those caring for you. As you develop others present more complex challenges. Through life you continually work out where you fit in to wider social groups (families and friendship groups, for example). Your sense of yourself grows. What's important to you develops in relation to others, as does your behaviour, your sense of identity and your political viewpoints.

Jürgen Habermas argues our motives are connected to things around us, including other people. He writes: 'the child reconstructively assimilates the social world into which it is born and in which it grows up. Complementary to the construction of the social world, there is a demarcation of the subjective world, the child develops its identity by becoming qualified to participate in normatively guided interactions.' For Habermas, we are interconnected with others and this social dimension is a part of our emerging sense of self.

How we learn to be moral beings

Think of questions your parents and teachers have asked from when you were small about how you treat others –

especially when they were correcting behaviour which could cause harm to others: How would you like it if someone punched you? What if someone broke your things? Should you push people? Can you please play nicely? Look at how well Molly is behaving!

In each case, a child is asked to think outside of himself or herself and imagine being the other person affected by his/her behaviour or asked to compare his/herself to the actions of another, whose actions are thought by an adult to be more praiseworthy. In this way a value system is reinforced via language and tone. This, along with other things, such as the stories parents tell children, establishes a code of behaviour for the child that will affect his/her interactions with others.

This is a homespun version of the ancient, golden rule or ethic of reciprocity: treat other people as you would have them treat you. Humans are taught this rule in many ways from childhood, yet repeatedly break it as they go through life.

There is evidence that young children's moral responses to dilemmas vary between cultures. In an article about moral education, Dr Robin Banerjee recounts a research study by Miller and Bersoff which compared the responses of children in two countries to a scenario in which someone

> . . . is about to catch a train to get to his best
> friend's wedding, where he is due to serve as best
> man. But . . . his wallet and train ticket are stolen.
> He then sees the opportunity to steal a ticket from
> another person. Should he steal the ticket to get to
> his friend's wedding? . . . when faced with these
> kinds of dilemmas, Indians and Americans (aged 8,
> 12, and 21 years) differed in their choices. An

average of 84 per cent of Indians chose to meet their social obligations (e.g. to serve as best man at the wedding) even if it meant breaking a principle of justice (e.g. by stealing). But only 39 per cent of Americans tended to resolve the dilemmas in this way. This kind of evidence strongly suggests that children's beliefs about morality are at least partly shaped by the value systems of the society in which they are brought up.

There is a tension between observing responsibilities to others and living in such a way that we preserve our values and freedoms and protect ourselves from harm. Most human lives hang somewhere in that balance. It is no surprise really that cultural factors affect moral responses of young people. But, as global communications improve, young people may become more susceptible to influence on their values through the media. Indeed Carol Craig's book, *The Great Takeover*, shows the potentially negative impact advertising and materialistic values have on people's lives. In her TED talk on the topic Craig says 'These things have come to dominate our values and trump everything else. There are lots of things we could be paying attention to like relationships, caring, meaning, community service, duty, spirituality, learning, development, fairness, equality, tradition, respect for nature. But materialist ideas take over.'

Helping young people to form values that affirm deeper respect for others is part of education for sustainability. And events like the Olympics can help in this.

Olympic values: equality and diversity

Moments in which we recognise we are part of something bigger – a complex, diverse and large human race – can help define us as individuals, communities and even nations. In many modern societies, it has become unacceptable to put people down or deny their dignity, whether on grounds of race, religion, sexuality, or capability. Being aware of and respecting difference underpins modern citizenship.

The Olympics is a modern reinvention of an ancient institution. The growing phenomenon of para-sports is a sign of greater international awareness of disability and illustrates the widening of Olympic ideals to encompass all people. In recent times, disabled athletes have been able to compete in their own games. Indeed, in the Commonwealth Games (as shown in Glasgow 2014) para-sports are now fully integrated. Perhaps the increasing appeal of para-sports has something to do with recognising the struggle some people encounter simply to survive or be recognised.

Public support for the games shows acceptance that labels and stereotypes about disability can be challenged and disabled athletes can become role models for all young people.

Paralympic cyclist, Neil Fachie, is a visually impaired athlete who embodies the heights of human achievement. I was present at a recent talk to students in a school, where Neil spoke about how achieving his gold medal at the London Paralympics was a culmination of years of work and an important part of dealing with his impairment. Stories like Neil's inspire others to achieve, and help us respect the merits of all athletes, regardless of physical capability.

The politics of the Olympics

It would be easy to get carried away by the emotional spectacle of the London games but this would be naïve.

43

There are problematic elements to some global wonders. For example, the Olympic Games are a multi-million dollar industry shaped by international political and economic processes. Dr Barbara Keys from the University of Melbourne argues:

> In the world today the Olympics are one of the most powerful cultural forces promoting a sense of global identity. Because the Olympics are the most accessible and emotionally resonant symbol of the global community, they can be said to represent a generally positive force. An estimated 60 per cent of the world's population watches part of the Games. It has unparalleled cultural influence . . . Olympic proponents say the Games promote international peace and goodwill, but the Olympics are often a tool for larger political forces, meaning they can be used for many political purposes, including cooperation as well as rivalry. International sport is always tied to politics. It's inescapable.

Some commentators also warn about the impact of the games on host nations' economies. An article in *The Economist* in 2013 highlighted the massive costs and also how they tend to attract the interests of politicians who see them as a vote winner. Another article in the *Washington Post* in 2014 argued corruption can cause costs to spiral and cited on Greece, whose economy collapsed after hosting the games. Of course, many factors led to the collapse of the Greek economy, but hosting the Olympic Games that cost over £9 billion was a contributing factor. Interestingly, the 2015 general election in Greece, showed how the country's economic collapse has led to a mood developing in the country to tackle the kind of economic injustice we will explore in a later chapter.

Thinkers such as Noam Chomsky question whether the alliance of corporate funders sits easily with the high ideals of the Olympic movement. In a disturbing blog, he wrote:

> On May 10, the Summer Olympics were inaugurated at the Greek birthplace of the ancient games. A few days before, virtually unnoticed, the government of Vietnam addressed a letter to the International Olympic Committee expressing the 'profound concerns of the Government and people of Viet Nam about the decision of IOC to accept the Dow Chemical Company as a global partner sponsoring the Olympic Movement.'
>
> Dow provided the chemicals that Washington used from 1961 onward to destroy crops and forests in South Vietnam, drenching the country with Agent Orange.
>
> These poisons contain dioxin, one of the most lethal carcinogens known, affecting millions of Vietnamese and many U.S. soldiers. To this day in Vietnam, aborted foetuses and deformed infants are very likely the effects of these crimes — though, in light of Washington's refusal to investigate, we have only the studies of Vietnamese scientists and independent analysts.

Chomsky exposes a darker side to the Olympics which is largely due to how the games are corporately funded. But there are also concerns about sporting integrity, given continuing suspicion athletes enhance their performance through drug taking. A recent *Guardian* article, based on research in Australia, claimed: 'Athletes as young as 12 are using performance-enhancing drugs in the hopes of emulating their idols, research shows.' BBC sports writer, Tom Fordyce, explains why even earlier drug taking is an issue: 'Research by University of Oslo scientists has established muscles can retain advantages given by anabolic steroids decades after the point at which they were taken.'

In short, many successful athletes could have used drugs at an early stage of their development, and so experience long term benefits without their drug use ever being detected. In fact, some scientists argue drug use is widespread. It is hard to get away from this. We simply do not know what we are watching when it comes to some elite sports. Allegations which surfaced in 2014, involving a number of prominent athletes, including 58 from Russia, have furthered this suspicion.

Events like the Olympics show what is possible in building relationships between countries and peoples, but more could be done. One of the people who realised their potential was Nelson Mandela. Once imprisoned for conspiracy to overthrow the state of South Africa, he gave an impromptu speech to South African athletes in 1992 at the Barcelona Olympics:

> All I want to say is that our presence here is of great
> significance to our country, a significance which goes
> beyond the boundaries of sport . . . Our country has
> been isolated for many years, not only in sports but
> in other fields as well. We are saying now, 'Let's
> forget the past. Let bygones be bygones.' I want to
> tell you that we respect you, we are proud of all of
> you and, above all, we love you.

Going beyond yourself. Identifying with others different from you. Being prepared to show kindness and love to others who have acted against you. In his Olympic speech, Mandela set a standard for humanity which turned respect into a form of heroism. At its best, this speech sums up the very best of what humans can aspire to through events like the Olympics. But, we would do well to consider such questions as:

1 Why do you think the Olympics inspires so many people?
2 How damaging are the negative aspects of the Olympics to its reputation?
3 How important is the Olympics to the project of developing a global sense of shared humanity?

CHALLENGE 2
Terrorism

You've seen the news images. Towers collapse as planes crash into them; people emerge wounded from wreckage of underground stations; rows of linen wrapped corpses lie riddled with chemically induced infection. Acts of terror can lead to feelings of outrage – making us feel others have behaved with a chilling lack of human feeling. We ask, how can they do such things?

The word terrorism is used to refer to acts of violence which can be perpetrated for a number of different reasons – such as religious or political convictions. Terrorism involves subverting someone else's human rights.

Some terrorist actions cause thousands of deaths. But sadly while we can feel outraged by such acts we can also quickly forget these tragedies which affect others. News ends. The channel changes. Mundane things take over. We resume our routines.

As time passes, we may not have the luxury of such attitudes.

The main difference between terrorism and war is that in terrorist activity ordinary people are prepared to take up arms for a cause, whereas traditional warfare has typically involved professional armed forces. It is easy to believe terrorist acts affect others miles away, but terrorism may threaten us all.

Some argue violence is a legitimate response to injustice. A recent *Time* magazine article defended rioting in Ferguson, Missouri, 'Peaceful protesting is a luxury only available to those safely in mainstream culture. When a police officer shoots a young, unarmed black man in the streets, then does not face indictment, anger in the community is inevitable. It's what we do with anger that counts. In such a case, is rioting so wrong?'

And, in 1961, a forty one year old Nelson Mandela gave a BBC interview asserting the importance of protest, including the possibility of violence, 'There are many people who feel it is futile for us to continue talking peace and non-violence against a government whose reply is only savage attacks on an unarmed and defenceless people. I think the time has come for us to consider, in light of our experiences, in this day at home, whether the methods we have employed so far are adequate.'

There is a spectrum of actions involving violence that cause terror, from rioting and looting, all the way to bombings on the scale of the Twin Towers. And of course there is a wide range of causes of resentment that might lead to these actions. Acts of violence in Ferguson seem to have emerged from a sense of injustice and oppression in the black community. This is a similar sentiment to the one Mandela expressed in 1961 in South Africa. By contrast, the bombings of al Qaeda were less about a spontaneous reaction to injustice, and more part of a global, strategic campaign based on an ideology. The similarity that exists in each case is in the root cause: a perceived sense of injustice; a wrong to be righted.

Terrorism and symbols

On November 11th, 2001, newspapers reported Osama bin Laden 'has for the first time admitted his al Qaeda group carried out the attacks on the World Trade Centre in New York.' It quoted bin Laden saying 'The Twin Towers were legitimate targets, they were supporting US economic power . . . What was destroyed were not only the towers, but the towers of morale in that country.'

Symbols like buildings can be important to terrorists. If you destroy something your enemy is proud of, or is represented by, you simultaneously weaken them and strengthen yourself. But human victims are also targeted. Terrorists want to make their enemy feel unsafe in their homes, towns and cities, so they threaten families and children – turning civilian areas into warzones. In their view the end they seek justifies the tactics they pursue.

Stories of victims

When Malala Yousafzai was fifteen a gunman boarded her school bus in Pakistan, shot her in the head and left her to die. He was a Taliban member and targeted Malala, who was campaigning for girls' education. The Taliban saw this as an attack on their beliefs. Malala survived and subsequently addressed an audience of 500 young people at the United Nations in New York. She said she has fought for women's rights because:

they are the ones who suffer the most. The extremists are afraid of books and pens. The power of education frightens them. They are afraid of women. The power of the voice of women frightens them. This is why they killed 14 innocent students in the recent attack in Quetta. And that is why they kill female teachers.

She won the Nobel Peace Prize in 2014. Also in 2014 *The Guardian* reported:

Residents in Chibok, in a remote corner of Nigeria's north-eastern Borno state, received phone calls warning them of an imminent attack from Boko Haram, the Islamist militant group. Residents in neighbouring villages had seen convoys with heavily armed insurgents heading towards the town, where a government school had specially opened for students to take final exams. A series of attacks on schools by Boko Haram – whose ideology opposes non-Qur'anic education – had forced mass closures in the state.

When the militants struck in the town, around 15 soldiers stationed in Chibok desperately held them off for almost an hour. But the soldiers were outnumbered and outgunned and no reinforcements arrived. By the time the assault ended almost five hours later, at least 300 schoolgirls had been carted away at gunpoint.

In both cases, young women receiving education became targets. This shows the challenge the international community faces in promoting equality. And also the extent to which some groups use terror to pursue ideas.

Rights of people in conflicts

War between nations is governed by Geneva Conventions –

rights agreed by the international community. The International Red Cross website explains:

> The Geneva Conventions and their Additional Protocols are at the core of international humanitarian law, the body of international law that regulates the conduct of armed conflict and seeks to limit its effects. They protect people who are not taking part in the hostilities (civilians, health workers and aid workers) and those who are no longer participating in the hostilities, such as wounded, sick and shipwrecked soldiers and prisoners of war.

Terrorists do not abide by such conventions: laws are forgotten, civilians targeted and enemies pursued to destruction. Torture and murder are tools.

This last point is important given recent admissions in the USA that authorities used waterboarding, a form of torture, on terror suspects at Guantanamo Bay. Barack Obama banned its use on becoming president in 2009 but in 2014, following a Senate investigation, he admitted the CIA had used torture. For many, this was a terrible admission by the President of one of the leading countries and it lessened the USA's moral authority in the eyes of commentators.

If national leaders do not respect Geneva Conventions they can be tried for war crimes. Former Liberian leader Charles Taylor was convicted by an international court. Former Serbian leader, Slobodan Milosevic died before his trial concluded. Following World War II and investigations of the holocaust and mass exterminations in concentration camps many Nazis were convicted for war crimes.

Conflict becomes terrorism when ordinary civilians become targets. But, in reality, things are rarely so black and white. Recent studies of civilian deaths as a result of conflict in Iraq (2003–2011) show how ordinary people are affected by war. Research carried out in the USA and Canada showed, 'more than 60 per cent of the estimated 461,000 excess deaths were directly attributable to violence, with the rest associated with the collapse of infrastructure and other indirect causes. These include the failures of health, sanitation, transportation, communication and other systems.'

For the purposes of this book, I have kept war and terrorism separate. But there is clearly a point at which the lines between them become blurred. Especially, as in recent times, western nations have explicitly conducted a 'war on terror.'

Essential human rights

The Universal Declaration of Human Rights was agreed in 1948 following World War II. It was drafted by international experts and provides a list of articles nations should observe. Indeed they should be supported by their laws. Human rights were to ensure, 'freedom, justice and peace in the world.' They included right to education; to freedom of speech; to support from law in cases of injustice; to belong to a country, and of asylum from persecution.

In their book *International Law*, Wallace and Martin-Ortega say: 'Generally human rights are regarded as those fundamental and inalienable rights essential for life as a human being. Human rights were born out of the need to protect the individual from the abuse of state authority.'

The first article of the declaration states: 'All human beings are born free and equal in dignity and rights. They are

53

endowed with reason and conscience and should act towards one another in a spirit of brotherhood.'

At some stage, humans developed a greater facility for thinking than other species. We learned to control our environment: made tools; farmed the earth; built shelters to protect our families and ultimately bigger, safer communities. Mark Pagel in his TED talk argues that the development of the 'social technology' of language was crucial to our development.

Language changed the nature of humanity. Consciousness of the environment around us, and of ourselves, is a part of what makes us human. And this awareness led to the idea of human rights.

At its most human level, citizenship comes down to how I treat you and how you treat me – about how we think of ourselves and other people.

United Nations' record on Human Rights

The UN is responsible for overseeing human rights and, in theory, member nations sign up to it. It has a Human Rights Council to which countries are elected. The Council has a Commissioner who reports on issues worldwide. But at times countries with poor human rights records have been elected to this Council. At other times the Commissioner has criticized nations for human rights' violations.

At a briefing to the UN Security Council, Commissioner Navi Pillay challenged countries: 'Short-term geopolitical considerations and national interest, narrowly defined, have repeatedly taken precedence over intolerable human suffering and grave breaches of and long-term threats to international peace and security.'

The right to vote

An example of a human right not always observed by nations is: 'The will of the people shall be the basis of the authority of government; this will shall be expressed in periodic and genuine elections which shall be by universal and equal suffrage and shall be held by secret vote or by equivalent free voting procedures.'

Many countries do not allow their populations to vote, despite signing the declaration. The Economist Intelligence Unit reports annually on the progress of democracy. In 2013 there were 25 full democracies, 54 flawed democracies, 36 hybrid regimes and 52 authoritarian regimes. This covers 167 countries, but not 'micro states'. 'Slightly less than one-half of the world's population lives in a democracy of some sort, although only 11 per cent reside in full democracies. Some 2.6bn people, more than one-third of the world's population, still lives under authoritarian rule (with a large share being, of course, in China).'

In a perfect world we would not need a Declaration of Human Rights, nor a United Nations to defend it. And countries would always treat citizens respectfully. But the world is not perfect. Every day people suffer rights abuses. So, we need to keep raising people's awareness of human rights.

Courage to be

Some of the greatest acts of courage have been in defence of human rights: Rosa Parks, Mahatma Ghandi, Aung San Suu Kyi are individuals who are synonymous with such actions. Owen Jones counsels against seeing these figures in isolation, but rather as part of wider movements or social trends. In their different ways, they symbolise a struggle for rights that runs through human history. Having the courage to be yourself and to insist on your rights has been part of human development. Ghandi's words from 1942 convey the courage and sacrifice it can take to stand up:

> There is something within me impelling me to cry out my agony. I have known humanity. I have studied something of psychology. Such a man knows exactly what it is. I do not mind how you describe it. That voice within tells me, 'You have to stand against the whole world although you may have to stand alone. You have to stare in the face the whole world although the world may look at you with bloodshot eyes. Do not fear. Trust the little voice residing within your heart.

On a personal level, when people stand up to those who are bullying, or intimidating them, they are claiming their rights. And, when we treat people in ways that diminish human rights, we are doing something unacceptable.

Freedom fighters or terrorists?

Governments sometimes use the term 'terrorist' to label people who are fighting oppression. Malcolm X is one example from the USA. Nelson Mandela, celebrated internationally for his stance against oppression, was labelled a terrorist by the South African government. The Dalai Lama is also seen as a terrorist by Chinese authorities today. One person's freedom fighter can be another person's terrorist. The world will probably judge acts as terrorism depending on the harm they do.

Sometimes terrorists justify actions by comparing the power their opponents have to their own. Smaller groups fight much larger and more powerful opponents in unconventional ways. This is the reason advocates of guerrilla warfare often give when justifying their tactics for dealing with powerful opponents. However, Mahatma Ghandi's protests against British rule in India exemplify non-violent civil action.

Challenges and sources of hope

Chemical terrorism could be a real danger in future. One person could send a virulent pathogen by mail and poison hundreds of people's airspace. The same person could send a thousand letters thereby affecting a whole country. Ricin poisoning attacks have worked this way in the past. The Unabomber did something like this in the USA in the 1990s, with letter bombs. Additionally, state sponsored killing without any due legal process has become a cause of international concern recently. A UN Report of 2013 raises some important questions about whether drone strikes, such as those carried out by the USA in countries like Pakistan and Yemen are legal. This is despite the fact the Obama administration believes such actions are a legitimate response to dealing with a terror threat posed by individuals. With such destruction at our disposal, human survival may depend on working towards an increased regard for the importance of human life.

As relief from this rather depressing picture, I offer the last word on this topic to Nelson Mandela, who after release from 27 years in prison said:

> When I walked out of prison, that was my mission, to liberate the oppressed and the oppressor both. Some say that has now been achieved. But I know that that is not the case. The truth is that we are not yet free; we have merely achieved the freedom to be free, the right not to be oppressed . . . For to be free is not merely to cast off one's chains, but to live in a way that respects and enhances the freedom of others. The true test of our devotion to freedom is just beginning.

Mandela's altruism following imprisonment is, for many, one of the great human achievements of the twentieth century. He expressed a spiritual world view which refused to be consumed by revenge or bitterness. His words and actions modelled behaviour he wished to see. His dignity showed respect for himself and others. He aimed to coexist with those he disagreed with and expounded a higher ideal of what it means to be human.

Some questions for you to consider might be:

1 Do you agree it is acceptable for Ferguson rioters to use violence to react to injustice?
2 Do you think the actions of rioters is different from acts of terrorists?
3 How can we promote respect for human rights successfully throughout the world?

Genetic Engineering

Now we turn to the micro-building blocks of life itself.
One of the most remarkable scientific breakthroughs of the
last half century has been the progress made in understanding the genetic make up of living things.

All human beings have an information code written into
every single cell in their bodies – a genetic code, or DNA. It
makes up your genes, which are inherited from your
ancestors. It affects your physical characteristics.

Professor Robert Winston's description of DNA captures
the sense of scientific wonder it has inspired, writing:

> . . . if anything might make you catch your breath at
> the awesome intricacies of the universe, then it has
> to be the DNA molecule. Picture a spiral staircase –
> the classic double helix featured in virtually every
> popular book on the subject. The two strands of
> this spiral stairway are strands of the sugar
> deoxyribose.

Winston describes it as a four letter alphabet in which all
life is written – the four letters referring to the four basic
compounds that make up all DNA. An elaborate biochemical
structure built out of simple components.

Most of our genetic make-up – 99 per cent to be precise – we share with other humans, but there is some variation to allow for difference to exist between individuals. These differences are essential for our survival.

In developing awareness of this code, scientists realised they might be able to use it to find cures for diseases or to affect the make-up of crops, for example. But scientific advance has brought with it controversies which show some of our fears of where science may be taking us. In this section, we look at the controversy surrounding genetically modified food in particular.

Science and fiction

Since the 1970s scientists have been researching and engineering genetic material. The decoding of the human genome, completed in 2003, allowed scientists to identify particular genes which predispose people to certain diseases and help them to find cures.

These developments happened in parallel to the cloning of the first sheep (Dolly) in Edinburgh in 1996. Dolly's birth led to public debates about the ethics of cloning. Should this technology ever be used to clone people for reproductive purposes? Or, to create human beings for families who could not have children, for example? Or should cloning be allowed for therapeutic purposes such as the creation of human tissues or organs for medical treatments? Should we clone human embryos?

In a TED talk, Paul Toot Wolpe says:

We are able to put technology into animals and
create organic robots. We are also able to use
organic material from animals to create computers.
We are creating creatures for our own purposes. We
can now grow human ears on mice to be
transplanted onto humans. Do we have free reign
to design whatever animals we want? Do we get to
create organic robots? When we start using these
technologies, what are the ethical guidelines? We
are directly designing the future of this planet.

On the other hand, Stewart Brand says synthetic hybri-
disation (using genetic modification to recreate extinct animal
species) would allow us to restore creatures destroyed by
human activity, 'Humans have made a huge hole in nature
over the past 10,000 years. We have the ability now, and
maybe the moral obligation, to repair some of the damage.'

Cloning seems like something from science fiction films
like *Jurassic Park*, *Star Wars* or *Blade Runner*. There are
genuine concerns about the ethics of cloning when it comes
to humans. Some even find it a revolting prospect. A
UNESCO report from 2004 gives a good overview of the issues.

But can we afford to ignore genetic engineering
particularly when these techniques are already proving useful
in medical research and treatment? In areas of medical
research, knowledge about the genetic make-up of people,
as well as technologies related to modification of human
cells, are coming together in emerging cures for things like
blood diseases and neurological conditions. There is hope
genetic research may yet help us find a cure for various
diseases including cancer.

Genetic modification of food

Public debate on GM food and medicines has been heated, leaving non-scientists confused at times. Indeed I'm aware making genetic engineering one of my Global Wonders risks a negative reaction from some.

Genetic engineering, or modification as it is sometimes called, means experimenting on genetic material and trying to affect it. In the popular imagination, such techniques are mainly associated with food. Food companies worked out pretty quickly that modifying the genetic make-up of a crop could change its properties, making it easier to grow or more productive. Those involved in agribusiness could also develop GM animals for food production purposes.

Early debates on GM crops in the 1980s and 1990s provoked such strong public reaction that crops were regulated across Europe and most of this is still in place today. Concerns were expressed about the impact GM crops might have on the environment and on people's health. However, Professor David Baulcome, a British plant scientist and geneticist thinks such regulations have led to inconsistencies and problems. Referring to a loophole regarding use of GM crops in animal feed, he proclaims: 'Bizarrely, our animals can eat GM, but we can't.'

In 2012 a survey, reported in *The Guardian,* indicated the British public were less worried about GM crops than in the past. The article also presents differing views on the issue. Caroline Lucas, Britain's only Green MP and former leader of the party, argued:

> If the government . . . thinks that this industry-sponsored poll is a sign of wholesale public

support for GM foods, then they are completely out of touch with reality. For decades, public opinion polls have consistently shown opposition to GM, not least because huge concerns remain about the environmental impact of this technology, the risks associated with cross-contamination for the future of non-GM food, and the dangers of placing ever more control of food production in the hands of big GM corporations.

The same article also quoted Mark Lynas, an environmentalist and author who was involved in ripping up GM crops in the 1990s and later became a supporter of the technology: 'Opposition to GMs was perhaps understandable a decade ago, but today it is a mistake. The science is clear that genetic modification in food crops is nothing to be scared of, and in fact can help address numerous environmental challenges, such as the need to raise yields whilst using less water, pesticides and fertiliser.'

This is the quandary environmentalists face with GM crops – science has moved on, but public opinion hasn't. Depending on your view, GM foods are either the 'most likely source of a new green revolution or (alternatively) as a disaster in embryo.'

Experts and commentators disagree. This is one reason why scientific advances can be difficult for lay people to understand and this not only creates a barrier for people, it also undermines trust, making it less likely the wider public will support those who argue genetic engineering has the capacity to solve some of the world's problems. What's more, great scientists are not always great communicators, so the public can easily get confused. Robert Winston writes:

> Humans do not find it easy to live with uncertainty
> and there is a growing perception in sophisticated
> societies, that our pursuit of scientific knowledge
> and its practical application is very dangerous. In
> the last ten years or so we in Britain have seen
> public suspicion of genetic engineering expressed
> in vehement protests by ordinary people about
> genetically modified crops.

Unless we develop a better way to share understanding about scientific development, human societies are unlikely to realise its full potential to help us.

Frankenfoods or high tech colonialism?

GM foods are sometimes referred to as 'Frankenfoods' in the media – alluding to Frankenstein's monster, a famous literary symbol of science going too far. But how might food change? You may be reading this, thinking you'd never put a genetically modified hamburger made in a laboratory in your mouth, but those who argue in favour of GM crops say that in future there may not be enough food to go round.

One argument concerns the inefficiency of meat production. The amount of food consumed by a cow, makes meat expensive in terms of money and use of natural resources. With an expanded human population, meat may become such a luxury that for some people lab produced burgers may be the only meat they can afford.

Genetically modified crops can be designed to survive in harsh climates, such as sub-Saharan Africa, where there is little water. Or they may survive in coastal conditions where salt resistant crops are required. These crops are sometimes called 'nutraseuticals'. If such laboratory derived crops can help to feed people who lack food, perhaps attitudes to them will change. Accepting them may depend on how much we trust producers and how far we perceive the crops to be beneficial.

While some worry about manipulation of food by major corporations, the science and technology journalist, Michael Specter, counsels against fearing change. In a TED talk, he says food production has always been shaped by cultivation and 'The idea that we should not allow science to do its job . . . is preventing millions of people from prospering. In the next 50 years we are going to have to produce 70% more crops than we do today.'

He also argues Western sensitivities about food modification interfere with necessary research which would help the poorest and hungriest people in the world. 'If we continue to act the way we are acting, we are guilty of high-tech colonialism.' For Specter, the rich withholding scientific advances from the poor is morally objectionable.

However, there is a counter-argument. George Monbiot made the following comment about food company Monsanto:

> An executive of the biotech company Monsanto said in 1996 that their aim was the 'consolidation of the entire food chain'," he says. "Monsanto quite overtly positioned GM as their means of achieving that goal, and it was quite a clear battle-plan that they had an aggressive patenting regime, patenting technologies and genetic material.

There is a conundrum here. Big business will drive a lot of the food research that can make a difference. And this may lead to developments that might help people in countries with food shortages. But there is often public mistrust of such developments. The drive for efficient, cheaper products is treated with suspicion by a public which does not like food to be meddled with, whilst simultaneously ignoring the extent to which industrial process affects the foods it habitually buys.

Phil Hanlon and Sandra Carlisle, in the first book in this series, identify an irony and a pattern, 'With our identities largely constructed around consumption, the economic system exploits the very crisis that it creates by proffering its various goods as solution.'

In recent years, there has been a cultural backlash in relation to food in some countries, with greater emphasis placed on locally sourced, organic foods. This is partly a reaction to commodification of food and actions of large food corporations and supermarkets. However, for everyone to live this way, there would have to be large scale systemic change and also a huge change in people's behaviours. Also, there is a question as to whether such an approach would be sustainable in feeding the entire human population.

Nobel Prize winning biologist, Norman Borlaug said in 2002:

> We can use all the organic that is available, but we aren't going to feed six billion people with organic fertilizer and we would level most of our forests... If we try to go back to low yield agriculture, we would have no option but to clear more land.

Mark Lynas, a convert to GM crops, argues there is a difference between how technology is controlled by big business and technology itself. He thinks a GM crop is simply a technology. He argues being against GM crops is a bit 'like saying I'm against tractors'. Ultimately he believes GM could save lives:

> In Missouri, they're growing GM cassava, which is an important food crop for 300 million people in sub-Saharan Africa. The cassava that's being grown in Africa is being hit by a viral infection that's sweeping across the continent, so a major threat to food security. There's no way a resistant strain can be made by conventional breeding – it's a bit like vaccination, in that a tiny bit of viral DNA is put into the plant genome, and you can't do that with selective breeding.

Food economics and future learning

With up to twelve billion humans to feed, we may have to live with the reality of lab produced burgers, chips made of GM potatoes and perhaps even recycled salads. More idealistic notions of sustainable living on local produce wherever you live might have to be sacrificed to the greater good of feeding the many – especially as there will be many mouths to feed and a strategic approach to food production might help societies to cope with demand.

Though a recent article on the Worldwatch Institute website argues organic farming worldwide could still be the solution.

> A seven-year study from Maikaal District in central India involving 1,000 farmers cultivating 3,200 hectares found that average yields for cotton, wheat, chili, and soy were as much as 20 percent higher on the organic farms than on nearby conventionally managed ones. Farmers and agricultural scientists attributed the higher yields in this dry region to the emphasis on cover crops, compost, manure, and

other practices that increased organic matter (which helps retain water) in the soils. A study from Kenya found that while organic farmers in "high-potential areas" (those with above-average rainfall and high soil quality) had lower maize yields than nonorganic farmers, organic farmers in areas with poorer resource endowments consistently outyielded conventional growers. (In both regions, organic farmers had higher net profits, return on capital, and return on labor.)

The economic and financial aspect of how big business operates should not be ignored, just as Big Pharma controls medicine supplies for profit, and Big Oil controls energy supply for profit, so multinational food corporations will do likewise with regard to GM food. People understand that businesses create jobs and wealth, but the sheer size and ambition of multi-national companies makes it difficult for them to build public trust.

Peter Melchett, policy director of organic farming group the Soil Association said recently, "The fact is that no tests are done to check whether GM food is safe for people to eat. Not a single British supermarket has said they will buy GM crops and sell them, and British consumers remain just as opposed to GM food as ever."

We will have to decide what is important to us and what we find an acceptable process of food production. We probably need to be more aware and to ask more questions. Public concern about scientific and corporate interference in the food chain needs to be aired in debate.

Ian Goldin and Pascal Lamy agree scientific confusion is a problem:

'From fracking to famine and from poverty to pandemics, scientific advice has never been in greater demand, nor has it been more uncertain and contested . . . Scientific uncertainty, an absence of consensus, and unclear relations between cause and effect are too often excuses for inaction . . . In meeting global challenges and considering the prospects for future generations, we must be tolerant of uncertainties. It is the balance of evidence—not least on the implications of inaction—rather than the certainty of outcomes that should inform our judgments.

In a TED talk Naomi Oreskes argues that we can trust scientists:

And this led the sociologist Robert Merton to focus on this question of how scientists scrutinise data and evidence. And he said they do it in a way he called organised scepticism. And by that he meant it's organised because they do it collectively. They do it as a group. And scepticism because they do it from a position of distrust. That is to say the burden of proof is on the person with the novel claim. And in this sense science is intrinsically conservative. It is quite hard to persuade the scientific community to say yes, we know something, this is true.

Perhaps the relative newness of the science involves just means that this conservative process of achieving consensus has not yet happened.

Genetic engineering shows both the wondrous and problematic nature of a particular scientific discovery. If it can be harnessed, it could be part of a revolutionary approach to tackling poor health and hunger. But the systems we have in place to harness it are part of the problem. Perhaps this all shows we need better science education, as well as more awareness of how large corporations use genetic engineering for profit. We need to debate some big questions:

1. Should moral objections to genetic engineering of food, or of human beings be allowed to stop these technologies from developing?
2. How can the public be protected from scientific advances they remain to be convinced about?
3. Can we rely on systems that promote profits for large corporations to solve food, health and energy issues we will face in future?
4. How can we make sure the poorest in the world are not victims of the hi-tech colonialism Michael Specter warns of?

Disease (Pandemic)

One of the greatest threats to continued human existence is a global disease with the power to kill large numbers of people. Such diseases might take many forms but the development of HIV shows how susceptible human beings can be to viruses. It has been devastating for various countries, mainly in Africa. AIDS is the final, and often fatal stage, of HIV infection.

AIDS is a 'pandemic' – it is spread throughout the world and not confined to one area. The World Health Organization estimates since it was first discovered in central Africa in the 1970s over 30 million people worldwide have died from AIDS. It also estimates in 2013, 35 million people were living with AIDS. The countries most affected are in the tip of southern Africa: South Africa, Zimbabwe, Botswana, Swaziland and Lesotho. In these countries 15–25 per cent of people aged between 15 and 49 are infected.

Disease like AIDS can cripple countries in part because they decimate professions such as police, doctors, teachers and nurses. In effect, the disease rips through nations' social fabric and systems for health, education and economies. It also crosses borders, exposing the fragility of states.

Growth of AIDS

AIDS is transferred via body fluids of people who have the virus. For example, you can get AIDS through contaminated blood transfusions or unprotected sex. Experts think HIV/AIDS have probably been around for several decades, but in the 1980s it became an epidemic and then a pandemic.

AVERT.Org reports on the extent of the problem:

> In Swaziland, a small landlocked country in Southern Africa, one in four adults are living with HIV. Since the first cases of AIDS were reported in the country in 1986, the virus has spread at an alarming rate and now Swaziland has the highest HIV prevalence in the world at 26 percent.
>
> HIV and AIDS have had a devastating impact on the country; particularly among families and households, with 6813 adult and child AIDs-related deaths in 2011. According to latest figures, life expectancy is just 48.9 years – one of the lowest in the world.

Reports show it is making progress in getting to grips with AIDs. But the UN recently recorded its concerns that Swaziland's existence as a country might be threatened if it does not deal with its AIDS epidemic.

AIDS also has had an impact beyond Africa, in Central America and North America, for example, as well as Caribbean and European countries.

Uganda

Uganda appeared to have tackled AIDS, achieving remarkable results. A UN Commission Report in 2012 stated: 'In Uganda, the national average adult HIV prevalence reduced from a high of 18.5 per cent in 1992 to about 5 per cent in 2000 due to, among other reasons, strong political leadership, open approach to combating the epidemic and a strong community response.' This supported an earlier 2005 WHO report.

In recent times, however, more people have contracted the disease. One contributing factor is complacency. Initially fear of the disease led people to live differently, but as time passes fear lessens. Current campaigns focus on reminding people of risks. By and large, deferring sexual activity and taking care in sexual relationships is good advice for everyone as it can help people, particularly young people, avoid sexually transmitted disease, including AIDS.

Annie Lennox

Scottish singer Annie Lennox is a UN AIDS ambassador. She is also an envoy for Scotland. She works throughout the world to raise awareness of the disease and promote actions that will help eradicate it. Providing support for victims is a key part of her work.

In a TED talk she highlights the case of an African girl born with AIDS, due to her mother carrying the virus. The child almost died and only survived due to improvements in medicine which allow her to live with a good chance of a healthy life. Annie Lennox argues 'every mother and every child in the world has the right to access good nutrition and good medical care.'

Lennox raises an important question in relation to global citizenship: how much responsibility do we have for other human beings, on a planet of seven billion people, when they live 6000 kilometres away?

Philosopher, Peter Singer, argues for effective altruism. He says we have responsibilities for improving the mortality rate of all children. He quotes UNICEF figures which show 6.9 million children died world-wide in 2012:

> Does it really matter that we are not walking past them in the street? Does it really matter that they are far away? I don't think that it does make a morally relevant difference that they are not right in front of us, the fact that they are of a different nationality or race . . . What is really important is; can we reduce that death toll?

So the big question Singer poses is: Can we distance ourselves from suffering when it is geographically remote from us? Is a child suffering in Uganda any different to a child suffering in the next street?

AIDS and the human condition

AIDS spreads through sexual activity and affects some groups in society more easily than others. This has led to certain groups, such as homosexuals being demonized as they are more at risk.

AIDS as a pandemic also showed the fragility of humanity as a species to attack by such viruses. AIDS in the 1980s was like a modern bubonic plague, decimating nation states, devastating systems and destroying health, security and education professions.

'Big Pharma' and government corruption

A key issue humans will have to address is the extent to which we can leave it to business and the marketplace to resolve social and health problems we will face. A key test of this relates to vaccines for disease.

In 2012 film maker Dylan Gray made a documentary which explored the story of how large pharmaceutical companies have exploited medicine patents to drive up profits and the consequence this had for millions suffering from diseases in poorer nations.

It is easy to believe companies put profits before humanitarian concerns. Despite this, *The Guardian* reported in 2012, 'Pharmaceutical companies are doing more to help people in developing countries obtain the drugs they need, according to the latest Access to Medicines Index.'

But, it is not just the actions of business which are in question. Distribution of medicines by government agencies in some countries which have need of medicine has also affected the supply of drugs. Corruption by officials is also a problem. The recent story of how Ukrainian officials were inflating prices of medicines as part of a government orchestrated scam can both affect the treatment experienced by sufferers but also public trust.

To deal with disease, we are going to have to find ways to ensure medicines are developed at reasonable prices, and supplied effectively to those who need them. Governments and businesses need to be held to account by some kind of process to oversee this.

New diseases

Unfortunately, new disease strains are difficult to predict and we just don't know when and where the next one will take effect until it does. For example, the Ebola virus has killed thousands and has spread beyond its initial epidemic source in Africa.

Virulent diseases are more likely to occur as the human population expands, the gap between rich and poor widens, and the risk of bio-terror grows. It may become even harder for large sections of the population to access health care and medicines they need. Tackling new infectious diseases might be crucial to our human future.

Michael Specter remains positive, 'In the rich world, some of the diseases which threatened millions of us just a generation ago no longer exist, hardly.'

How we deal with the most vulnerable tells us about the state of our species. Different countries have different levels of resilience when it comes to facing pandemic. One issue that may become more pronounced as the human population expands is the extent to which access to medicines is available to the poorest people in the world.

Some questions to consider might be:

1 How should we protect people from pandemic diseases?
2 How freely available should access to medicine be?
3 How can we manage the needs of commercial business in relation to producing medicines?

WONDER 4

Telecommunications

In a Ted talk entrepreneur and founder of the X Prize,
Peter Diamandis, argues a burgeoning population is a source
of hope, especially in 'connecting to the global conversation.
These people will inject tens of billions of dollars into the
global economy. They will bring contributions we cannot
even predict. The biggest protection against a population
explosion is making the world healthy. We are now more
empowered than ever because of new technology.'
Diamandis demonstrates the kind of scientific optimism which
sees future challenges largely as technical problems to solve.

There is little doubt the internet, which so many people
now access in homes and on mobile devices, connects us
with people everywhere. The United Nations' specialised
agency to monitor telecommunications reported in 2014 that
of seven billion people in the world, 40 per cent are using
the internet – almost three billion users. It also claims by the
end of 2014 there will be seven billion cell phone
subscriptions world-wide.

How we use technology

In the past twenty years there has been a mobile technology revolution. In a TED talk Amber Case claims 'we are all cyborgs now'. She defines cyborg as: 'an organism to which exogenous components have been added for the purpose of adapting to new environments.' She argues, 'tool use for thousands of years has been a physical modification of self – to go faster, hit things harder – and there has been a limit to that. But now what we are looking at is not an extension of the physical self, but the mental self. And because of that we are able to travel faster, communicate differently . . .'

Amber Case describes the increasingly intuitive way we interact with technology to enhance life. Indeed humans may be in the early stages of adaptation to physically incorporate technological components. If this sounds like science fiction, think about how many devices we currently rely on: phones, MP4 players, and tablets. Think also about how we plug into them and how they are designed to fit with our bodies and lifestyles.

In future we will have access to super computers which may outstrip human capacity for thinking. Machines may organise larger areas of human life. Life may involve more interaction with technology – we are perhaps on the path to becoming a species of human-cyborg.

A digital echo from *Heart of Darkness*

In the late nineteenth century, Polish exile, Joseph Conrad wrote one of the finest novellas in the English language – *Heart of Darkness*. It described western exploitation of the Belgian colony of the Congo for rich ivory resources which were used for jewellery and European cultural entertainments, mainly piano keys and dice. To get highly prized ivory, European traders not only sacrificed elephants for their tusks they also subjugated native populations. Conrad showed savagery is part of the human make-up and Western civilisation merely masks that truth.

We like to believe we have moved on from Conrad's day, yet the following story from the same region, over 100 years later, has a nagging similarity. Nowadays it's not ivory that is exploited but something with a similar type of connection to entertainment in wealthy nations.

How much do you love your mobile phone?

Did you know that every mobile phone or tablet relies on particular natural resources to make them work? One of these is called Coltan. This is a kind of rock which contains the element tantalum, crucial to the building of tantalum capacitors in electronic devices. Mobile phones, tablets and games consoles contain such a component, which means we are surrounded by tiny amounts of this material. If we use these electronic devices then we are consumers of tantalum, even if we do not know what it is, where it is from, or what exactly goes into its production.

There are not many places where this substance is mined, but one is the Congo. Mines are run by armed groups which control workers by force and employ children as cheap, exploitable labour. They work long hours in dangerous conditions, at risk of serious injury or death. Female workers are subject to rape and abuse. Children are used as soldiers to guard the mines.

In a TED talk Bandi Mbubi tells why he became a refugee from the Congo. For him the phone may be a 'symbol of an interconnected world, but it leaves a bloody trail.' He claims 'since 1996 over five million people have died in the DRC [the Congo]. Countless women men and children have been raped, tortured and enslaved. The quest for this mineral has fuelled this war.'

Bandi Mbubi also points to an irony: as workers now have mobile phones, they can send information to the wider world about conditions in the mines. 'The mobile phone has given people an important tool towards giving people their political freedom . . . The mobile phone is both an instrument of freedom and oppression.'

The exploitation of African resources Conrad exposed a hundred years ago in *Heart of Darkness* is being revisited in the form of mobile technologies. Mbubi demands fair trade mobile phones so that those mining Coltan are unharmed. Sadly this seems a long way off.

Phones, social media and democracy

The mobile phone allows us to speak to strangers around the world. In 2011 there were a number of uprisings in Arab countries such as Tunisia, Libya and Egypt. In these events, ordinary people documented their experience through reportage and photojournalism, often captured on mobile phones, and then broadcast to the world via social media.

Evgeny Morozov, a writer and technology specialist, cautions us to see 'digital tools are simply, well, tools', and points out 'social change continues to involve many painstaking, longer-term efforts to engage with political institutions and reform movements.'

Many commentators proclaimed the Arab Spring as an example of the power of social media. But as Professor Ramesh Srinivasan points out there is some scepticism about such claims:

> Some argue that social media empowered activists to coordinate and communicate the actions that sparked the revolt. Others, in contrast, argue that social media was a double-edged sword, and in some cases prevented activists from directly confronting the old regime. Skeptics point out that regimes are effective at using technologies to spy and subvert.

In some cases state monitoring of citizens' internet use has led to arrest and punishment of people, whose actions were considered to be seditious. For example, eleven social media users in Iran were arrested for making insulting comments about a religious leader online.

Two experts on globalization, Ian Goldin and Pascal Lamy detect a growing problem:

> Governments are realizing the significance of social media as a potent communications tool . . . In countries like Egypt, Tunisia, and Yemen, social media has been widely credited for its role in the downfall of dictatorships during the Arab Spring . . . Citizens are now able to raise issues and mobilize in protest more quickly and easily than ever before, yet the complexity and plethora of issues has weakened the capacity of governments to respond speedily. New capabilities of leadership are required, able to manage public expectations,

uncertainty, rapid change, and an increasing complexity of issues.

Improved tools for communications present challenges in terms of how human societies will organise themselves politically. Social media can allow ideas to be shared simply and easily, and as a result create difficulties for existing social and political orders. People may expect more as a result of being more aware of issues. The pattern of increased political engagement and expectation for example was formented on social media during the recent referendum on Scottish independence. Conversely, governments may be able to exert more surveillance over people through these self-same tools.

The amazing expanding and shrinking world

In 490 BC Pheidippides ran 25 or so miles from Marathon to Athens to inform people of the city they had successfully defeated the Persian army in battle. He promptly died from his effort. In the 1800s, Napoleon's semaphore system allowed messages to be relayed between Paris and the 'fringes of the country in a matter of three to four hours'. In 1844 Samuel Morse sent the first coded message through an electric telegraph between Baltimore and Washington – the first instantaneous message transmitted over distance.

Developments in telephony and televisual communication have ensued since then. In the early twenty-first century individuals have the capacity to reach people in other countries through a range of media, expressing complex feelings and ideas.

Global population is expanding, but connectivity is better. We have more chances to befriend people in other countries.

For humanity to survive, we probably have to harness this power and find ways to build communities across nations, endowed with purpose.

With technological progress, digital literacy is an issue for us to address. The internet requires a capacity to read and write – something millions of people worldwide do not have. This shows the importance of basic education programmes as well as encouraging development of digital skills.

Optimists about globalisation place faith in learning, science and technology. They think we can evolve and acquire new ways of doing things. In that context, telecommunications is a real global wonder. Jamie Drummond even thinks we can use social media to 'crowd source the world's problems'.

Some important questions might be:

1 Should there be such things as fair trade mobile phones and tablet devices?
2 What changes might telecommunications and devices make to human lives in future?
3 What changes might be made to ways governments work as a result of telecommunications innovations?

Human Population Expansion

One argument we have heard is that GM crops may be important because of the number of people there will be on the planet.

In an essay, American writer, Gore Vidal wrote, 'At the time of Confucius (the fifth century BCE philosopher) China was underpopulated; yet all of the ills of society were blamed on overpopulation: "When men were few and things were many," went the ancient saying, "there was a golden age; but now men are many and things are few and misery is man's lot."'

These words seem appropriate for our own time of 7 billion people, with even more pressure on "things" or resources being felt around the world. Especially when UN projections for population growth by 2100 suggest there will be many more human beings in the world, unless there is a catastrophe. Positive estimates suggest the population plateaus at around 8 billion and starts to shrink. More conservative projections see it rise to 10 billion by 2100. Whereas, if current growth is maintained, we could have a human population of over 12 billion. This would probably be catastrophic.

In 2002 Jean-Francois Rischard, former Deputy of the World Bank, used international research to highlight twenty global problems. His main worry was the anticipated increase in population, a 'demographic explosion': 'More than 95% of the 2 billion people to be added over the next two decades or so will live in developing countries. . . With this population increase and with higher living standards in the developing world, the world's food production will have to increase by over 40% over the next twenty years.'

The evidence Rischard drew on came from an international team of scientists. Over twenty years the International Panel for Climate Change has developed a body of statistical evidence that causes concern, even if people have taken opposing views about what it might be telling us.

Rischard's book is still worth reading, even after twelve years. Further reports from the IPCC seem to confirm the validity of problems he identifies. In a later section this is discussed in detail.

A quick way of getting your head around the nature of the global human population as it stands is through the 100 People Organisation. It gives an overview of human culture at this point and the extent to which people suffer social and economic hardship. It also provides a context for Millennium Development Goals.

Progress and population

The expanding human population is partly a tribute to scientific advance, notably improvements in programmes of health and diet, including medicine. In a TED talk, Swedish statistician Hans Rosling shows in the last fifty years average family size has reduced globally but life expectancy has increased, 'Life expectancy and family size are now almost exactly the same in Vietnam as in the USA, whereas at the end of the Vietnam War, they were very different. This shows Vietnam has caught up. As for poverty, there is much less poverty in Asia than in the 1970s.'

Rosling's talks promote optimism. He charts improvements in health and social conditions over the past few hundred years. He explains the impact of family planning on certain nations in Africa and Asia, and of inoculation programmes to tackle diseases which had devastated certain countries. Such factors have helped countries to improve the quality of life of their citizens.

But, as population expands to a critical point, our capacity to control our environment may be overwhelmed by the sheer volume of people we need to sustain. The very successes Rosling highlights have created a major problem – an increasing, aging population we need to look after.

More people living longer creates a need for different kinds of care for the elderly than in the past – and much more of this care is needed. This pressurises communities globally, creating a challenge for the future.

Of course, when there are too many people, resources needed to feed and water them become scarce. People are drawn to large communities like cities where there is the possibility of work and better services. However, city life brings increased likelihood of disease, which spreads more quickly when people live more closely together. As Rischard pointed out, the number of cities of over five million people is projected to grow considerably over the next generation.

Understanding the population problem

Stephen Emmott says humans are the source of the greatest threats to our survival. He quotes alarming statistical evidence to support his claims. A *Guardian* article by Chris Goodall disputes some of Emmot's statistics and presents what he claims is a more balanced view. Both writers are worth reading to get a flavour of the debate between those who are either pessimistic or optimistic about the future.

In fact, UN figures show 1.2 billion people live on less than $1.25 per day (classified as Extreme Poverty). Subsequent generations will need to contend with the needs of the increased population to eat and drink. They'll need heat and shelter. When they get ill, they'll need medicine. But will we have enough resources on the planet to satisfy the different needs of so many? And how should we work as an international community to tackle poverty and hunger for the increasing number of poor people?

There are three basic scenarios we might aim to consider in relation to international health, poverty and hunger when contemplating the great numbers of people in the world who are suffering due to lack of resources. First, poorer people and nations can be brought up to the level of wealth and resource of wealthier ones. Or, wealthier people and nations may have to sacrifice wealth and share more. The third option is that we just accept the growing gap between rich and poor and the inequalities this leads to. Interestingly, Millennium Development Goals establish objectives in tackling poverty and inequality, showing a willingness in the international community to help those most in need.

Speaking in his TED talk about industrialised nations, like the USA, Alex Steffen says:

> if everyone on the planet were to live the way we do, we would need five planets worth of resources. We don't know yet how to build a society which is environmentally sustainable, which is shareable with everybody on the planet, which promotes stability and democracy and human rights and which is achievable in a timeframe which is necessary to make it through the challenges we face.

It is perhaps unsustainable to increase the level of consumption for the poor to those of the rich. There is probably not enough to go around, given population projections. Phil Hanlon and Sandra Carlisle suggest that in future we will all have to consume less. But currently international economic systems are driven by consumption and these would have to change dramatically for that to transpire. Some commentators argue there may be negative economic consequences in allowing this gap to persist.

Promoting environmental sustainability

One Millennium Development Goal is to ensure global environmental sustainability. This responds to concerns about the habitat of the planet and its ability to support a rapidly growing human population. And also the point at which the expanding population means a shortage of essential resources (food, water, energy). Additionally, we need to get real about waste and its potential effects on particular areas and on the wider planet.

In 2001 Green Party MP, Caroline Lucas, who was then a Member of the European Parliament, wrote a paper called

'Stopping The Great Food Swap, Relocalising Europe's Food Supply' which explored some rather absurd facts about international trade in food:

> Britain imports 61,400 tonnes of poultry meat from the Netherlands in the same year that it exports 33,100 tonnes of poultry meat to the Netherlands. Britain imports 240,000 tonnes of pork and 125,000 tonnes of lamb while exporting 195,000 tonnes of pork and 102,000 tonnes of lamb. Why?

Jonathon Foley explains in a TED talk 'we face one of the greatest challenges in human history. The need to feed nine billion people and do so sustainably, equitably and justly. At the same time protecting our planet for this and future generations. This is one of the hardest things we've ever done in human history. And we have to get it right in our first and only try.'

Michael Specter agrees, 'Vaccines, modern medicines, our ability to feed millions of people are triumphs of the scientific method, which is one of the great accomplishments of humanity. Despite our triumphs, a billion people go to bed hungry.'

In a later section, I consider energy – an issue closely related to the kinds of products consumed in wealthy nations. It takes a lot of energy to make and move goods for consumers. While many jobs are created through this, it is not necessarily sustainable. Perhaps, when fossil based energy is less available, people will have to live more locally and sustainably. This in turn might lead to more equity and less waste.

You can end up feeling depressed by the challenges facing humanity. However, Robert Winston speaks for many when he says 'I don't believe we're doomed.' Whether or not it leads to doom, population increase will change the nature of life. We may experience greater gaps between rich and poor, pressures on resources and vulnerability to disease.

A few questions that may be important in the next century are:

1   At what point will the earth be over-populated by humans and how will we recognise we are at that point?
2   What responsibilities do we have to others in the world and how should this affect how we behave?
3   How can we organise the human population to consume less, whilst maintaining important freedoms for people worldwide?
4   Should we take steps to limit the human population? And if so, what would these be?

CERN

CERN is the European Agency for nuclear development.
It has been engaged in the last ten years in one of the most
incredible scientific projects of modern times and has made
history in the process. It is best known for the Large Hadron
Collider.

Some modern scientific concepts have so outstripped the
knowledge of the lay person, it is difficult for most of us to
take part in some debates about our technological future.
The Large Hadron Collider at CERN in Switzerland is a
massive research project that has a purely scientific goal at
its heart. But there is much more to it than that and some of
this has been quite surprising.

Humans have used nuclear technology to power cities with
electricity and to create weapons of mass destruction.
Nuclear energy contains enormous power and physicists are
still exploring its potential. It involves understanding the
tiniest of particles of matter that make up existence. How
these particles behave under pressure helped scientists
create powerful technologies. This is where CERN comes in.

The CERN website gives the following information:

The Large Hadron Collider (LHC) is the world's largest and most powerful particle accelerator. It first started up on 10 September 2008, and remains the latest addition to CERN's accelerator complex. The LHC consists of a 27-kilometre ring of superconducting magnets with a number of accelerating structures to boost the energy of the particles along the way.

Inside the accelerator, two high-energy particle beams travel at close to the speed of light before they are made to collide . . . The electromagnets are built from coils of special electric cable that operate in a superconducting state, efficiently conducting electricity without resistance or loss of energy. This requires chilling the magnets to -271.3°C – a temperature colder than outer space.

Again, the statistics are amazing – like they have been taken from a science fiction story. But the superconductor exists and real scientists built it.

In the 1950s a theoretical physicist at Edinburgh University, Professor Peter Higgs, came up with a theory explaining the origin of the mass of elementary particles and confirmed the standard model of particle physics which scientists had been working on for decades. Since then, scientists have been on a quest to find what they called the *'Higgs Boson'*. In 2012 scientists at CERN successfully identified a Higgs Boson type of particle, thereby proving fifty years of theoretical science had real value.

The problem of science and public understanding

As a result of CERN experiments, scientists believe human knowledge has advanced. In 2013 Peter Higgs and his colleague, Francois Englert, were awarded the Nobel Prize. However, few members of the general public could claim to understand the science – or indeed what it actually accomplished. What's more, there is no particular immediate usefulness to the discovery. And it cost billions of euros to accomplish. So why bother doing such work?

Robert Winston gives a good response when he writes '. . . of the ten greatest inventions of the last fifty years none of those inventions were goal orientated. Nobody set out to design the laser. Nobody set out to design a microchip that would actually change the way we communicate. . . And so we have to recognise that it is basic, non-goal orientated science that is important'.

CERN has increased human understanding of factors which shape the universe. One goal was to resolve a scientific problem relating to how laws of physics operated at the beginning of time. There is no way for us to know if this will lead to practical applications.

But sometimes science produces spin off developments, by-products of the main goal. Tim Berners-Lee, a British scientist working at CERN, developed a system for scientific communication across the world. This became the World Wide Web. Out of pure scientific research at CERN came an amazing product that revolutionised life – a mechanism for mass international communication by ordinary people. Perhaps people should think about the power of the internet and how it has transformed their lives when they question the value of pure scientific research.

Robert Winston highlights an important paradox. On the one hand, science makes most progress when it is not goal orientated, but simply about exploring an area of interest for its own sake. On the other, humanity has particular goals it needs scientific minds to address – such as Millennium Development Goals.

To return to an earlier analogy, in this respect science is like a quest to a new place no-one has visited before.

Myths about CERN and anxieties about science

In 2008 newspapers reported some scientists wanted to stop the experiments as they were concerned about their potential consequences. An article in *The Independent* stated:

> Some scientists . . . went to the European Court for Human Rights to try to stop the collider being turned on. They fear it may create a black hole – which would certainly violate our rights by sucking the planet into . . . well we don't really know. Professor Sir Chris Llewellyn Smith of CERN says: 'The chance we produce a black hole is minuscule.' Which is not all that reassuring. But he adds: 'Even if we do, it can't swallow up the Earth.' It would be too small, and disappear in moments. In any case, they will only send the hadrons in one direction this week. The collisions start in October. Until then, at least, we're not all doomed.

Elaborate sci-fi type conspiracy theories played out in the press, to the bemusement of the public. One concern was the collider would facilitate an invasion of earth from the future. When the collider experienced delays some scientists postulated that mechanical problems could be because it was sabotaging itself from the future. As far as we know, neither of these scare stories was true.

In 2012, at the successful conclusion of experiments, Professor Incandela, a senior scientist involved said, 'We're reaching into the fabric of the Universe at a level we've never done before' adding 'We're on the frontier now, on the edge of a new exploration. This could be the only part of the story that's left, or we could open a whole new realm of discovery."

And perhaps this is the problem – we are exploring a realm of unpredictable scientific development. We simply do not know where it will lead. And we do not know how much we can take on trust from researchers.

Science as a threat

Robert Winston accepts science has produced technologies worrying to the public. These concerns encourage some to ask whether constant scientific advance is 'a good thing'. They believe science is out of control. Nuclear power is an example of a technological advance which benefits humans as an important sources of energy, yet which disturbs many. Winston believes the way round this is for scientists to show the usefulness of the science they are developing. However, he appreciates sometimes this can be difficult.

One recent example is the Measles, Mumps and Rubella vaccine which one vocal medical researcher claimed was dangerous to children's health. Scientists and politicians failed to get their case across in a confusing media campaign. As a result some parents chose not to have their children vaccinated and many contracted diseases as result. Some of these illnesses can prove to be fatal.

Winston also argues scientists 'may need to find a new compact with the public . . . Better science literacy is the key. We need to find ways of communicating more effectively with people who are not scientists and to recognise the ethical limits of what we are doing.' Winston's manifesto for scientists establishes a code for research and communication of developments.

Technological citizenship

In the next eighty years, humanity will have to deal with some man-made problems, themselves a consequence of scientific activity. Industrial processes have created biodiversity losses in some parts of the world. Think about the logging of vast areas of rainforest for export in South America, or Malaysia; the effect of chemical pollution on fish populations; and the number of species being lost globally as the human population grows.

Science as a process is perhaps not as widely understood by the general public as it needs to be. Perhaps we need to find different ways of educating people about the science that is part of their lives – and through school curricula emphasize the relationship between science and citizenship.

This makes our relationship with science a complicated one – a bit like having a friend who sometimes does things that stop you trusting him or her, and who can get you into trouble, but who is nonetheless interesting to hang around with.

In fact, it is difficult to blame science for some of the uses that we have made of it. It was a non-scientist that ordered the dropping of the atom bomb, after all.[27] To return to our troublesome friend analogy, it is probably true to say we have encouraged, or even goaded, that friend to do ever more dangerous things on our behalf. And now we may have to live with the consequences.

Some questions to ask might be:

1 What lessons can we learn from CERN?
2 How can such international projects help humanity in future?
3 How do we manage concerns of the public about such research?

Future Resources: Conserving our Habitat

As we saw earlier, the human population has been rising rapidly for a number of years and is projected to increase further in the next century. Stephen Emmott writes: 'An increasing population accelerates the demand for more water and more food. Demand for more food increases the need for more land. Increasing demand for food also increases food production and transportation. All of these accelerate the demand for more energy.'

This places further pressure on the planet's resources. We eat more and use more water and energy. There are also consequences for other species. The World Wildlife Fund estimates between 2000 and 10,000 species are lost every year. In the last thirty years butterflies, frogs, birds and types of tigers and leopards have become extinct. We simply do not know what the loss of species (both plants, insects and animals) means for the planet's eco systems. The WWF talks of an extinction crisis which is man-made.

This theory suggests human beings affect the environment and destroy other species at an alarming rate. Humans seem incapable of protecting elephants and rhinos from being hunted and rainforests from being stripped, or stopping species dying out when the natural habitat is affected by humans.

Resource depletion

We risk running down the planet's resources in a number of areas. Expert on sustainability, Jonathon Foley examines how the planet's resources will have to stretch to meet the needs of a growing population, arguing certain things we are accustomed to having today may become luxuries in future. Foley explains the amount of the earth's resources that goes into agriculture just to feed human beings:

> So we have this incredible presence today of agriculture dominating our planet. Whether it's 40% of our land surface, 70% of the water we use, 30% of our greenhouse gas emissions. We've doubled the flows of nitrogen and phosphorous around the world simply by using fertilizers, causing huge problems with water quality from rivers, lakes and even oceans. And it's also the biggest single cause of biodiversity loss. Without a doubt agriculture is the single most powerful force unleashed on this planet since the ice age. No question. And it rivals climate change in importance.

Foley still thinks agriculture an 'absolute necessity' and that we will have to do much more of it to feed a larger population. Feeding people sustainably is the challenge.

The Guardian reported in 2013, 'The majority of the 9 billion people on Earth will live with severe pressure on fresh water within the space of two generations as climate change, pollution and over-use of resources take their toll, 500 scientists have warned.'

The article also quoted UN Secretary General, Ban Ki-moon, who told delegates at a science conference in Bonn, 'We live in an increasingly water insecure world where demand often outstrips supply and where water quality often fails to meet minimum standards. Under current trends, future demands for water will not be met.'

Human activity has an impact on oceans and on fish stocks. But pressures on supplies of drinking water also emanate from human pollution and waste. Quite simply our current activities are storing up problems for future generations.

There is potential for human catastrophes such as droughts and 'water wars'. History shows powerful nations have colonised other peoples to exploit certain resources. It is not too far-fetched to imagine countries waging war to control fresh water supplies, or fishing territories, or sub-sea energy resources. As Rischard said, 'Water deficits are building towards a major planetary challenge . . . Control over water could become a frequent cause of international conflict, particularly where there is a history of antagonism.'

Fish conservation

A number of popular species, including cod and haddock, are in danger of extinction. Fish farming can also create other problems such as disease.

Humans rely on fish to feed our ever increasing populations, yet we risk destroying that basic natural resource. We need to an international approach that the problem of conserving fish and to ensure that their fishermen understand and respect agreements about when and how much to fish.

Interestingly, the updated European Union Common Fisheries policy emphasises conservation of stocks by fishermen. From the fishermen's point of view, policy making has to reflect their views as well and make sense to them. Environmental groups like Greenpeace place responsibility for overfishing at the door of large industrial fishing companies.

Waste, contamination and water scarcity

Toilets are perhaps not the most appealing topic to bring up in general conversation. But we need to confront the issue of human bodily waste. It takes a lot of water to remove human waste from domestic toilets and also to process it in sewage treatment plants.

Carl Hensman works in the Water, Sanitation and Hygiene team at the Gates Foundation and writes: 'The average person in the United States uses around 80–100 gallons of drinking water EVERY DAY and most of that ends up in the sewer to keep the sewer system functioning properly.' Given the mounting shortage, water is not being well used. There is not enough water to provide such sewage treatment for everyone in the world now, with current population levels, let alone in the future, when there will be many more people. So, your poo is part of a mounting global problem.

Waste water pollutes natural water supplies if not carefully treated. So too does industrial pollution. Poor sanitation leads to disease such as diarrhoea, which kills around 760,000 children each year. We need to manage waste, while improving sanitation and maintaining supplies of drinking water. Controlling pollutants is part of the solution.

Nonetheless it's not sustainable for us to continue using water as we do today.

Investment in technological improvements like water filtration systems (which NASA claims as a spin off from space science) might help. But, lack of fresh water resources will remain one of the biggest global problems.

Planning for future energy needs

Rob Hopkins is a co-founder of the Transition Network. He argues when people consider future energy needs there are some typical responses. However, what he describes is not just confined to energy and applies to other areas of resource depletion as well.

Hopkins describes the first response as seeing the future as essentially the same as the present, but perhaps a bit more pressurised – 'a sort of business as usual model.' The second response is to think there is little hope and we are probably doomed.

The third response is the position of more optimistic advocates for science. According to this view we can invent our way out of problems through improved technologies and communications.

The fourth is what Hopkins calls 'the Transition approach' which prepares for a world which no longer relies on fossil fuel. This is the response of Hopkins and his Transition network. He argues the lack of planning for a fossil free future is a major worry:

> . . . we are coming towards a time when our degree of oil dependency is our degree of vulnerability. For

every four barrels of oil we consume, we only discover one. And that gap continues to widen. The amount of energy we get back from the oil we discover is falling. In the 1930s we got hundreds of units of energy back for every one we put in to extract it. Already that has fallen to 11. There are 98 oil producing nations in the world, but of those 65 have already passed their peak.

I am sitting in the city of Aberdeen as I write this – the oil and gas capital of Europe and a boom town. Prominent figures in the oil and gas industry dispute Hopkins' analysis. They say there is continuing oil and gas resource to be tapped and are optimistic about future off-shore oil production. They argue technologies will improve, helping production and reducing cost.

The energy market is changing. At the time of the Scottish Independence Referendum in September 2014 oil traded at $115 a barrel. By December 2014 it had dropped to $70 and some predict it could drop to below $60 and stay there for a number of years. The price drop is partly due to battles for market share among oil producing nations and different policies on production by countries like USA (which is importing less oil) as well as a slow-down in the global economy, which led to falling demand for energy.

In Scotland the argument about oil has largely been about how much there is, but the issue is more about the cost of recovering it and whether it is worth it given oil prices are now low. However, despite the economic needs of Scotland, it should also be remembered oil is a fossil fuel and it causes damage to the environment when it is burned. If we are committed to reducing carbon emissions, we cannot continue to burn more and more oil.

Hopkins argues our survival as a species depends on how we deal with energy issues – since society's systems depend on energy. To transport food between countries, you need fuel. To drive high-tech industries, you must have energy. To heat homes and work places you need an affordable source of power. If fuel runs out, or costs too much, the way we all live will change.

Physicist Steven Cowley sees nuclear technology as the answer to future energy need. This is a controversial opinion as many are opposed to nuclear energy and few want to live near a reactor. Nonetheless Cowley points out, 'As we try to lift billions of people out of poverty, we are using energy faster and faster and the resources are going away. The way we will make energy in the future is not with resource, it's really from knowledge. If you look fifty years into the future, the baseload energy drivers will be: fusion, fission, solar.'

Food we eat. Water we drink. Homes we live in. Transport we use. Even the air we breathe. All of these have the potential to become a source of international concern in the next hundred years.

Ian Goldin argues 'A new awareness will have to arise of how we . . . mobilize ourselves in a new way and come together as communities to manage systemic risks. It is going to require innovation and an understanding that the glory of globalization could also be its downfall. This could be our best century ever, or it could also be our worst.'

One risk is that nations use force against each other to secure increasingly scarce resources. Fareed Zakaria writes:

> Do these countries want to live in a world entirely ruled by the interplay of national interests? Since

1945, there have been increasing efforts to put in place broader global norms — for example, against annexations by force. These have not always been honored, but, compared with the past, they have helped shape a more peaceful and prosperous world. Over the next decade or so, depending on how rising new powers behave, these norms will be strengthened or eroded. And that will make the difference between war and peace in the 21st century.

Some questions for us might be:

1 Is it right for some people, particularly in economically developed nations, to consume so much when others have so little?
2 How can we make the drive of companies for profit compatible with the project of conserving our natural resources?
3 How do we reverse the process of depletion of our natural resources, in the context of an expanding human population?
4 How do we balance national interests with global issues?

WONDER 6
Electronic Gaming

Some people may think it controversial to include gaming as a Global Wonder. But recreational use of computing technology is a phenomenon that has changed how human beings spend their free time. Things we can do now would have been unthinkable a generation ago – and is perhaps part of a wider adaptation human beings are making, using technology to enrich experience.

Broadcaster, Charlie Brooker, began as a gaming journalist and has written extensively on the development and impact of gaming. For him, explaining gaming to those who have no interest in it is difficult.

> Try as they might, video games still don't seem to really register in the mainstream "old media". Newspapers and television still largely report on the gaming world as though it is something mildly amusing that happens overseas. Statistics about how many billions the industry is worth, or how many billion players there are worldwide, tend to be recited with an air of amused disbelief. It's almost as if video games only exist in the imagination of a few friendless dreamers.

He also says, 'If you don't play games, you're not just missing out, you're wilfully ignoring the most rapidly evolving creative medium in human history.'

Those who *get* gaming are involved in a high-tech world that those who don't are bemused by. For Brooker, to be a gamer is to be part of a club that can be quite exclusive when we are talking about some of the more elaborate games now available:

> It's not just wilful ignorance on the part of rusty old media. It's hard to make games interesting in print or on TV, especially to non-players. Compared to other popular artforms, there aren't many "personalities" in games; no George Clooneys to interview or Britneys to pap. What's more, when addressing a casual audience, it's incredibly hard to describe what a game actually consists of. The majority of people don't speak the lingo. Everyone understands terms such as rom-com or thriller, but mention first-person shooters or MMORPGs and you might as well be speaking Gaelic . . .
>
> End result: for all the talk of just how many trillion units Modern Warfare 2 has shifted, games strike around half the population as utterly inaccessible: a peculiar situation for a mass-market industry.

For Brooker, gaming has had a meteoric rise, is a technological marvel and an art form. But it has perhaps left some people behind. To that extent, it symbolises the electronic revolution: it proceeds at pace; offers great opportunities – but if you don't keep up, you may be excluded.

Twenty-first Century wonder

The history of gaming is short. From the earliest stages of the home computing boom which took hold in the late 1970s, gaming was a part of the package. From the rudimentary tennis game Pong, played on early consoles, and arcade platform games, like Space Invaders, gaming evolved in tandem with available technology.[4]

In the 1980s, games were uploaded from coded cassettes to home computers. CD-ROMs emerged a decade later. Now, we download them to phones or consoles – or play on-line. Charlie Brooker's film, *How Videogames Changed the World*, shows the transformation in technology and the impact games had on people as they developed to their current sophistication.

Games consoles now facilitate high specification graphics and allow an impressive range of experiences. Different genres of games exist: Shoot 'em Ups, strategy, role play, sports – and those involving car theft on a grand scale in urban USA. Some consoles have been developed to facilitate group and family interaction, to address the perception that gaming is antisocial – the Wii exemplifies this best. In the era of smart phones, people carry mini consoles around in their pockets and play in free moments.

Technology is evolving to meet burgeoning recreational demands. The Entertainment Software Association reported that US consumers spent $21.53 billion in 2013 in America alone. Their research showed 59 per cent of Americans play video games and that on average there are two gamers in each American household. They also claim that 51 per cent of US households own at least 1 console, computer or mobile phone. The average gamer is 31 and has been playing for 14 years.

Gaming has also affected twenty-first century cinema. Film character Lara Croft began life in video games. Films like *Tron* depict action inside the world of a video game. Avatar included an element of strategy and role play in a scenario that seemed to have been drawn from the world of gaming. In future, there may be more and more interactive experiences that combine both media. Interestingly, gaming makes more money than films.

Use of computer generated graphics to enhance visual experience moves film towards the realm of gaming. And, recently there have been many films with superhero characters that facilitate gaming scenarios. Kids watch Batman at the cinema and then go home and play the game on a console.

Some people even consider gaming a sport. Colleges are starting to give eSports scholarships and eSports tournaments are held with million dollar prize pots and large on-line audiences. Simon Parkin writes:

> But the emerging world of professional video game competition – or eSports – is serious business. This year's Call of Duty tournament has a prize purse of $1m[14] and the winning team takes home $400,000. Elsewhere, last year's prize pot for the fantasy-themed League of Legends championship – arguably the most popular online game in the world today – was $2m,[15] attracting sponsorship from heavyweight brands such as Coca-Cola and American Express.

Pros and cons of gaming

Some commentators have concerns about how intense game playing by young people affects social interaction in families. *The Economist's* Babbage blog recently commented:

> There is ample evidence to suggest that people are spending more time playing games. They are also spending more on them. The video game industry is among the fastest growing sectors of America's economy and generated $25 billion in sales in 2011. Children between the age of eight and 18 play video games for nearly 15 hours a week in the country. Some studies have identified that 8% of gamers are "pathological players" . . . Whatever the precise figure, it is clear that a small proportion of players are addicted. Such pathological gaming is associated with depression, anxiety, social phobia and, in children, impaired school performance.

However, the article balances these concerns, 'The benefits of gaming, however, should not be overlooked. Games have been used to train people to type, to overcome phobias, develop motor skills, teach problem solving, release tension and even exercise. A brand new study suggests they might help those with dyslexia learn to read.'

Gaming provides experiences which promote learning. Unlike cinema which is more passive, gaming allows personal agency. Players orientate themselves in alien environments and perform tasks. Games are challenge based and encourage organisational skills which are useful in everyday life.

Grand Theft Auto

Grand Theft Auto is one of the biggest grossing global games. It is produced in Scotland by Rockstar North. It is hugely popular and equally controversial. Scenes of violence provoked a ferocious moral reaction and an equally ferocious defence.

Peter Hitchens wrote a *Daily Mail* article on the subject:

> If the Devil had his own bible, it would probably take the form of a computer game. It would be sly and witty, enjoyable and slick. It would start with small, almost funny misdeeds.
>
> It would offer the player the joys of money, successful violence and easy, responsibility-free sex. There would be drugs which didn't fry your brain or burn holes in your nose.

In *The New Statesman*, Member of Parliament, Tom Watson responded:

> Thankfully – despite what Peter Hitchens might think – gamers understand satire. And Grand Theft Auto Five is one giant targeted missile of satire locked on to the superficiality of media, commerce, celebrity and politics . . . As I write this, I realise how hard it is to describe the game to you. You just have to play it in order to understand the comedic depth of the world you enter when you switch on your console . . . Every feature, from the flickering streetlights and unique advertising hoardings to ambient noise and radio station playlists, has been painstakingly woven into the experience . . . There is room for legitimate criticism of GTA V, but politicians and commentators will have to work much harder to understand this creative medium before they can be taken seriously by gamers.

Controversy also affects other games. In 2009, the BBC reported a dispute between Tom Watson and another MP Keith Vaz, about the game, Modern Warfare II:

> Keith Vaz, the Labour MP for Leicester East, who said this: "I am absolutely shocked by the level of violence in this game and am particularly concerned about how realistic the game itself looks."
>
> Mr Vaz has been a long-term critic of the games industry, and plans to raise his concerns over Call of Duty in the Commons this afternoon in questions to the culture secretary and his team.
>
> But within hours another Labour MP Tom Watson had hit back, "Are you sick of UK newspapers and (my fellow) politicians beating up on gaming? So am I. The truth is, UK gamers need their own pressure group. I want to help you start one up.

The big issue is violence. But *The Independent* recently reported on a long term US study on effects on young people of playing violent games. It concluded there was no link between gaming and violent behaviour. It should also be said, though, that a body of academic research compliled by academic Karen E. Dill and others over the short period of gaming suggests a correlation between gaming and tendency towards addiction and violence. She concludes, 'Many top-selling videogames have harmful content and therefore cause negative social effects. However, videogames are popular with youth and have many characteristics that make them excellent teaching tools.'

An OECD report from 2007 states:

> Although the existing evidence does not offer conclusive answers to questions regarding the effects of different uses of technology on the social development and behaviour of young people, it

indeed indicates that its potential harmful impact cannot be overlooked.

Perhaps we should continue to be aware, and hopefully tackle some of the potential risks associated with gaming. In so doing, we are more likely to enhance its benefits.

Gaming and citizenship

Jane McGonigal gave a TED talk on how gaming is a means to promote democratic attitudes. For her, games like 'World of War Craft' provide inspiration:

> If we want to solve problems like poverty, hunger, climate change, obesity, I believe we need to aspire to spend at least 21 billion hours a week playing games on line by the end of the next decade.' That isn't too far-fetched as she quotes statistics that show children in the USA currently spend as much time gaming as they do in school.

McGonigal says gaming involves intense concentration on solving problems. She co-developed a game called *Superstruct* which requires players to collaborate to solve problems facing the world.

Such an altruistic vision of gaming contrasts with the marketing objectives of gaming companies. Some people worry when big business targets young people and contributes to a materialistic culture that can adversely affect them. There are also concerns games can contain the imaginations of young people, rather than release them. Alternatively, as McGonigal argues, gaming creates opportunities for creative thinking that could benefit the next generation.

Scandal of *Angry Birds* and global espionage

The influence of gaming in the contemporary world was shown in the Wikileaks scandal. Edward Snowden has become notorious or heroic, depending on your view. Some see him as a champion of ordinary people's rights not to be spied on by their government. In this view he is seen as a whistle-blower. Others see him as a traitor to his country.

Snowden was a US army employee who leaked secret information through Wikileaks – a website devoted to providing the public with information about how governments behave. Snowden's leaked data showed the US government had engaged in long term surveillance of ordinary people.

A 2014 *New York Times* article alleged that spies were using people's personal data from apps, like *Angry Birds* (a gaming phenomenon downloaded around two billion times, the equivalent of a quarter of the human population). Gamers provided information about their age, gender and sexual preference:

> The N.S.A. and Britain's Government Communications
> Headquarters were working together on how to
> collect and store data from dozens of smartphone
> apps by 2007, according to the documents, provided
> by Edward J. Snowden, the former N.S.A. contractor.

A recent IPSOS international poll showed how this could happen. More than half of 16,000 people surveyed world-wide did not check terms and conditions before signing up to web products, such as games.

A problematic wonder?

It is a world-wide phenomenon; a technological marvel. Its violence either concerns people; or is an ironic commentary on modern life. If you get it, it is life enriching; if you don't, it is a turn off.

Gaming shows that use of technology is increasingly intuitive. Its defenders highlight its potential to harness our creativity. Its ability to engage young people is a strength. In future, we will see more elaborate technologies, allowing more complex experiences. Perhaps gaming can be part of the solution to global problems, as Jane McGonigal suggests.

Some questions for us might be:

1 How much does electronic gaming affect your own life?
2 How can the learning people acquire through gaming help them in other areas of life?
3 What potential might there be in gaming to transform human societies?

CHALLENGE 6
Climate Change

In 2002 Jean-Francois Rischard published a book called *High Noon*, based on work of the International Panel for Climate Change. It outlined twenty critical global issues such as the depletion of global fisheries due to overfishing, to the melting of polar ice caps due to global warming.

Rischard argues that tackling global issues will require international cooperation on a scale not previously seen by human civilisation. Solutions require a radical approach: intense, collaborative action across nations. Rischard argues democratic processes are themselves part of the problem as they lead to short term thinking by politicians and this militates against longer term strategies which are essential if we are to counter climate change.

Scientists and commentators

In the past few years a great deal has been written about climate change, making it a difficult issue to cover. Some experts claim the world is getting unnaturally hotter due to human activity – and that climate change is a global crisis. Others say rising global temperatures are part of a natural cycle. No wonder people can feel confused. Undoubtedly we worry about the numbers of natural disasters, such as hurricanes and tsunamis. But disagreements between scientists and scientific commentators have left people perplexed about whether or not global warming is happening at all and whether it is connected to human activity.

When Al Gore produced the film *An Inconvenient Truth* in 2006, there was a strong reaction from many in the scientific community who disagreed with him. In September 2013, following another report by the IPCC, environmental commentator, George Monbiot blogged:

> Already, a thousand blogs and columns insist the Intergovernmental Panel on Climate Change's new report is a rabid concoction of scare stories whose purpose is to destroy the global economy. But it is, in reality, highly conservative.
>
> There are no radical departures in this report from the previous assessment, published in 2007; just more evidence demonstrating the extent of global temperature rises, the melting of ice sheets and sea ice, the retreat of the glaciers, the rising and acidification of the oceans and the changes in weather patterns. The message is familiar and shattering: 'It's as bad as we thought it was.'

The most recent IPCC report appears to have consolidated scientific consensus on the matter. The report is worrying. It describes and predicts rising sea levels, increased temperatures, more frequent extreme weather episodes and, most worryingly, damage to the atmosphere from carbon emissions that will affect the world for centuries to come. It states:

> Cumulative emissions of CO2 largely determine global mean surface warming by the late 21st century and beyond. Most aspects of climate change will

persist for many centuries even if emissions of CO2 are stopped. This represents a substantial multi-century climate change commitment created by past, present and future emissions of CO2.

Getting scientific agreement is a difficult enough step, but getting politicians to do something about it is much harder. There is some evidence that governments interfere to ensure the findings of the IPCC do not damage their economic interests, such as fossil fuel emissions. Some scientists feel that the alliance of corporate and political interest is stifling the research.

Journalist Nick Cohen writes:

The politicians know too well that beyond the corporations and the cultish fanatics in their grass roots lies the great mass of people, whose influence matters most. They accept at some level that man made climate change is happening but don't want to think about it.

I am no better than them. I could write about the environment every week. No editor would stop me. But the task feels as hopeless as arguing against growing old. Whatever you do or say, it is going to happen. How can you persuade countries to accept huge reductions in their living standards to limit (not stop) the rise in temperatures? How can you persuade the human race to put the future ahead of the present?

And that is the problem. People block out problems from their day to day lives – taking a 'We'll deal with it if and when we have to' attitude. A mixture of apathy, self-interest and confusion seem to be the biggest barriers. And yet, when young people engage in discussion, their fears quickly surface, as does their motivation for action. They worry about their futures and those of any children they might have.

Until there is a really compelling case for changing how we live, putting the environment first just won't be a high enough priority. It is easy to understand why politicians think there is too much to risk in telling us to radically change our behaviour. They are elected for a few years whereas the actions needed to achieve sustainability may not bear fruit for thirty years or more. It is also difficult for politicians to see past the next election because we demand immediate answers from them. The candidate or party promising to lower petrol prices, or increase available family budgets will usually defeat the politician with the best plan for a sustainable environment in fifty years.

You may worry that we are not thinking far enough ahead, or asking the right questions about our future. Perhaps our lack of appropriate action is storing up even bigger problems for our descendants. I certainly take this view and believe there should more focus on such issues in school.

Planning for the future

Some writers, like Steven Emmott see little hope for humanity. Others, like Rischard are more positive. Both recognize the tension between the interests of groups of people, or nations, and those of the planet as a whole.

The environmental dilemma is similar to the one facing us all when we plan our individual futures. Do we plan on the basis of what will make us happy in the short, or longer term? Do we focus on what will make us happy individually, or collectively?

Emmott argues that human beings are only likely to realise what actions are required when things become really difficult. He thinks it will only be when there are ten billion people on the planet and we are relentlessly harvesting rainforests and oceans for food resources, and everything is becoming much more expensive, that we will start to take notice. However, he argues that by then it will be too late to address problems.

While taking care to avoid the scaremongering that often accompanies debate on climate change, it is worth asking people to consider what kind of world they want to inhabit in fifty years' time. And also to ask them what they intend to do as citizens to ensure a positive future. No matter how many people there are in the world, we are in it together.

Iain Goldin and Pascal Lamy, experts on development, argue we are living at a unique point in history:

> We have come a long way since the catastrophic war of a hundred years ago. Indeed, we stand at a unique point in history. Our younger generations are the first to live free of the scars of previous global wars. Given extraordinary advances in knowledge and scientific understanding, we are more aware than ever of the implications of our actions on future generations; we can no longer plead ignorance, not least in areas like climate change and biodiversity. And we could arguably be among the last generations able to do anything to stop the long-term devastation of our planet.

Hope for the future

American educator John Hunter developed The World Peace

Game for children in Virginia, USA. They learn about peace and how countries might work to accomplish it:

> I was creating a lesson for students on Africa. We put all the problems of the world there and I thought, let's let them solve it. I didn't want to lecture or have just book reading. So I thought, let's play a game. I'll make something interactive and it has since evolved . . . We have ethnic minority tensions, nuclear proliferation, oil spills, environmental disasters, famine, endangered species, global warming – my fourth graders solved global warming in a week.

The engagement of young people in John Hunter's class in global issues is remarkable. If this work were to be part of the curriculum for young people internationally, perhaps it could help solve some future problems. For Jan Eichhorn, the recent referendum on independence in Scotland showed the potential of young people to become involved in political process. But, Andy Mycock argues it revealed important gaps in terms of the information and skills young people need to engage fully in such processes.

Naomi Oreskes expresses optimism that the required scientific consensus will transpire:

> Here is the paradox of modern science . . . actually science is an appeal to authority. But it is not the authority of the individual . . . It's the authority of the collective community. You can think of it as a kind of wisdom of the crowd, but a very special kind of crowd . . The collective work of all of the scientists that have worked on a particular problem . . . Scientists have a culture of collective distrust . . .

Perhaps our understanding of science needs to be better, so we can put into context the various disputes between scientists, and not simply mistrust them.

Some questions for us might be:

1 How can we help the public understand scientific lessons being learned about climate change?
2 What can scientists do to help public understanding?
3 What can be done to promote more effective education of students and teachers in this area?

The Universal Declaration of the Rights of the Child

Globally, the plight of women and children is inextricably linked. Important issues include: the education of girls; protecting children from abuse; risks affecting young mothers; early child development.

One of the most important Global Wonders is the 1959 Universal Declaration of the Rights of the Child. It is based on an earlier document from 1923. It subsequently led to the UN Convention on the Rights of the Child in 1989. The Declaration establishes the idea that all people, regardless of race, class, religion, gender or wealth have rights, and that all children have the right to receive free, compulsory education. Commissioners for young people exist in UN countries. In some respects these edicts on children were a continuation of the Universal Declaration of Human Rights, established in 1948.

UN declarations are unique documents which could not have existed in the past. They resulted from reflection in the international community following World War II. They focus on protecting and nurturing children, a key factor in sustaining human life.

Universal Children's Day takes place on November 20th. It was first proclaimed by the UN General Assembly in 1954 to 'promote the welfare of children throughout the world.'

Countries throughout the world are at different stages of development, culturally, socially and economically. You can tell a lot about a nation's progress from its attitudes to human rights – and to protecting children.

The Importance of childhood

UNICEF says childhood, 'is a precious time in which children should live free from fear, safe from violence and protected from abuse and exploitation. As such, childhood means much more than just the space between birth and the attainment of adulthood. It refers to the state and condition of a child's life, to the quality of those years.' Unfortunately, this aspiration is not always met.

The International Criminal Court was established partly to deal with those who use young people as child soldiers. In 2012 it delivered its first guilty verdict, against Thomas Lubanga, leader of the Union of Congolese Patriots, which controlled gold resources. He forced children as young as eleven to fight for him. Some were subjected to torture and rape. He is serving a fourteen year sentence.

Sir Harry Burns highlights the importance of early child development. Problems at this stage can lead to serious health issues later.

Developmental problems such as speech defects are commonly associated with some kind of neglect. Such problems should be a signal that something needs to be done . . . In essence what we have been seeing happen is children who live in chaotic circumstances are switching into survival mode, instead of developing proper executive functioning. The survival centres develop at the expense of the other bits of the brain. Chaotic and uncertain early years have a powerful influence on the full range of psychological and physiological systems. It takes longer to integrate new knowledge. It is harder for kids to learn if they have experienced this kind of uncertainty.

UK statistics reveal '50,000 children are currently at risk of abuse . . . One in four young adults were maltreated during childhood. Between one and four children die every ten days in the UK due to child abuse.' These figures are sourced from the NSPCC and show an on-going need to protect the rights of children.

Save the Children recently reported on the effect of poverty on childhood in Scotland and found when children from poor backgrounds start school they are:

- almost twice as likely as other children to have difficulties with their physical development
- twice as likely as other children to face difficulties with their emotional development
- 50 per cent more likely than other children to face difficulties with their social development
- 40 per cent more likely than other children to face difficulties with their cognitive development
- twice as likely as other children to face difficulties with their communication development

The evidence is clear: many children who grow up in poverty in Scotland are starting school at a serious disadvantage to their classmates.

By the age of five, the gap between rich and poor has already determined the parameters in which children might achieve.

Millennium Development Goals – education

The Declaration on the Rights of the Child also informed Millennium Development Goals – especially those focusing on education of girls and young women in less developed nations.

The United Nations MDG report shows that internationally the percentage of girls receiving primary and secondary education, compared to boys, is improving, though girls still lag behind, especially in later school years. Males are predominant at university level. In economically developed nations, women's involvement in tertiary education is often greater than men's. However, in less developed nations, women are underrepresented.

If fewer girls go to college and university, they have less opportunity to change their economic and social circumstances and are more vulnerable to discrimination. The right to an education is closely related to the economic power and social status people have. But an OECD report argues that education of women promotes economic growth:

> Increased education accounts for about half of economic growth in OECD countries in the past 50 years, and that has a lot to do with bringing more girls to higher levels of education and achieving

greater equality in the number of years spent in education between men and women.

If women do not access education equitably, there will be an effect on their ability to participate in the workplace. This is a vicious circle that can only be addressed by getting more girls a better education.

In a TED talk, author Sheryl WuDunn describes the plight of a girl called Dai Manju in rural China and the expectations many parents there have that girls' education is an unnecessary expense: girls don't need to be educated as their life will be spent working in the rice fields. By gaining her degree Dai was able to buy her parents a better house with water and electricity thus showing the transformative power of education on families. WuDunn argues if you invest in education, people can accomplish more. 'It is a waste of resources if you don't use people like Dai Manju', she says.

The barriers Dai Manju faced were cultural, relating to parental expectations. Engaging with education was not a priority for them. This may be quite common. It is, though, yet another example of the barriers people face in overcoming poverty – and international evidence shows this is harder for women than men.

For WuDunn the 'central moral challenge of this century is gender inequality.' Improving education for girls would be a significant step forward for equality and justice. It is reassuring that UN reports on progress towards Millennium Goals shows improvement is being made.

Violence against women and children

More troubling than inequities that exist between genders in education is more basic abuse suffered by women and children – especially the practice of genital mutilation. The World Health Organisation (WHO) estimates 140 million women and girls are affected worldwide with over 100 million of them over the age of ten in Africa. The practice is mainly performed at birth. In most societies where it is practised, it is a cultural tradition based on ideas of female modesty and sexual fidelity. In 2012 the UN passed a resolution to eliminate the practice.

The World Health Organisation recently appointed Dr Christine Kaseba-Sata as a Goodwill Ambassador, to highlight forms of gender based violence. She believes 'Women are not empowered. Women are subordinate. And for a lot of men, the issue of gender based violence is a show of power, flexing their muscles . . . And women are afraid to move on because they have no means.'

These are some fairly troubling examples of discrimination which can affect women. But the greatest form of discrimination might be to be denied life on the basis of gender. Madeleine Bunting writes:

> Half a million girls a year are being aborted
> in India, equal to the total number of girls born in
> the UK. The scale of sex selection in Asia is
> extraordinary, yet it has not attracted the attention
> it deserves in the west. This is the age of "missing
> women" – an estimated 30 to 70 million of them.

Indian economist and philosopher, Amartya Sen wrote: 'We can estimate the number of "missing women" in a country by calculating the number of extra women who would have been, if these countries had the same ratio of women to men as obtain in areas of the world in which they receive similar care. In China alone this amounts to 50 million "missing women".'

Elsewhere Sen argues the problem with missing women also 'relates to higher rates of disease from which women suffer, and ultimately to the relative neglect of females, especially in health care and medical attention.' In short, greater numbers of women than men die in some parts of the world because of social and cultural factors that lead women to experience poor health and to lack appropriate access to medical treatment.

Equality and justice

Poverty presents barriers to children, in places stopping them from accessing rights to education. However, in some countries there are even more fundamental problems. The rights the UN outlines for children are paid lip service to, or treated as aspirations, rather than entitlements.

Nonetheless it was a huge step forward for humankind to have a clear framework for rights and mechanisms through the United Nations to promote them. And there is evidence of progress towards Millennium Goals. But children do not automatically gain access to what they are entitled. A much greater human population, with possibly fewer basic resources, may mean more pressure on rights.

Some questions the international community needs to answer include:

1 How can we protect women and children from violence?
2 How can we promote more effective education for girls and women?
3 How can we ensure that children born in poverty receive a proper education that promotes their life chances?

CHALLENGE 7
Gap Between Rich and Poor

In the twenty-first century, people live longer and experience better health care. They generally are wealthier than in the past. But in recent times there has been a large number of books and articles published on the subject of the gap between rich and poor. The narrative emerging is that wealth is too concentrated to the hands of a few and that this is becoming a major challenge. The economist Robert Shiller is famous for having warned about impending bubbles in technology stocks and housing. He says 'the most important problem that we are facing now today, I think, is rising inequality in the United States and elsewhere in the world.'

The gap between rich and poor generates frustration and injustice. Professor Danny Dorling, a social geographer and expert on inequality, writes:

> Around the world, a majority of the global protests
> that have occurred since January 2006 have centred
> on issues of economic justice. In 2006 there were
> just 59 large protests recorded world-wide. In just
> the first half of 2013 there were 112 protests of a
> similar size. The rate of large scale global protest
> has increased fourfold in six years. And these

protests are "more prevalent in higher income countries." – countries where more of the 1 per cent live. Why is this?

Dorling cites the recent Global Wealth Report 2014 by Credit Suisse writing: 'Taken together, the bottom half of the global population own less than 1% of total wealth. In sharp contrast, the richest decile hold 87% of the world's wealth, and the top percentile alone account for 48.2% of global assets.'

The report also shows that there are around four million more dollar millionaires in 2014 than in 2013 and also projects that in the next five years there will be almost twenty million more. It says of trends in inequality:

As regards wealth inequality trends, our results for the whole period 2000–2014 show that wealth inequality rose in exactly half of the 46 countries monitored. Splitting the period reveals markedly different experiences before and after the financial crisis: inequality fell in 34 countries in the earlier years, but in only 11 countries after 2007 . . . inequality rose in China and India both before and after the financial crisis, and declined slightly in North America in both sub-periods . . . However, it is interesting to note that only one G7 nation – the United kingdom – appears in the list of 23 countries recording an increase in inequality this century.

The fact the top one per cent of the global population owns very nearly half of the wealth may not be fair, but there are also a number of potentially disastrous social and economic consequences that might result from it. In 2011 UNICEF reported, 'Not only does inequality slow economic growth, but it results in health and social problems and generates political instability.'

The same report notes women suffer poverty more than men:

> . . . the numbers of adult women and girls living in poverty are alarming. As of 2007, roughly 20 percent of women were below the $1.25/day international poverty line, and 40 percent below the $2/day mark. Girls and younger women also suffer disproportionately from poverty, as more than one-quarter of females under the age of 25 were below the $1.25/day international poverty line, and about half on less than $2/day.

It is difficult to read such information and not feel that human development as a project is not working that well for far too many people. The question for us is whether we wish to accept this situation or challenge it.

Authors of *The Spirit Level, Why Equality is Better for Everyone*, Richard Wilkinson and Kate Pickett note some consequences of inequality:

> We also showed that there is a large and consistent body of evidence on income inequality and violence . . .
> The weight of the evidence, and its continued rapid accumulation, make the important link between income inequality and social dysfunction inescapable.

Sir Harry Burns, former Chief Medical Officer for Scotland draws a link between the biological events that lead to poor health and low life expectancy, such as heart disease, and social psychology. In a TED talk, he explains the destructive force affecting the lives of the poor as:

a cycle of alienation that may begin with early years, leads to mental ill health in childhood, leads to behaviour problems at school . . . they fail in education, they end up often in prison, . . .

We think that if we fix poverty everything will be all right. Poverty is part of a cycle and poverty is often as much a consequence of this cycle as a cause of it. Action that is required has to happen across the whole of that life force. We have to deal with early years, we have to deal with teenagers, we have to deal with the health and young people who are being alienated even further, we have to help older people who become isolated.

He says the way forward involves collaboration to achieve shared understanding between practitioners and politicians and a shared commitment to changing the lives of children for the better. He gives the specific example of improving attachment between parent and child through reading bedtime stories and important early years collaborative work developing in Scotland.

The poor performance of the United Kingdom in relation to the growing gap between rich and poor has caused widespread concern because of its social, but also negative economic consequences.

Millennium Development Goals

In the year 2000, as part of the celebration of the millennium, the United Nations agreed eight areas of priority for action by 2015, called the Millennium Development Goals. The goals are:

- End Poverty and Hunger
- Universal Education

- Gender Equality
- Child Health
- Maternal Health
- Combat HIV/AIDS, Malaria and other diseases
- Environmental Sustainability
- Global Partnership

Specific goals for each of these topics are ambitious and measurable. They have helped countries to prioritise and plan. They have also helped to create a picture of how people are treated in specific countries. The goals are backed by finance from wealthy nations who commit 0.7 per cent of their Gross National Income to Overseas Development Aid.

There are encouraging signs we are making progress towards these goals. For example, research by statistician Hans Rosling shows significant achievements in improving education and treatment of women and also in tackling poverty. And in a TED talk, Iain Goldin highlights tacking inequality as a key challenge for humanity.

Literacy and inequality

It is probably no surprise that not being able to read or write can have a huge impact on people's lives. Statistics published by the National Literacy Trust show people with poor literacy are more likely to lead lives affected by mental illness and divorce and are less likely to have a career. In short, a person's literacy affects their ability to lead a fulfilling life.

The United Nations established the International Day of Literacy in 1965 to highlight a global problem. Many people in the world cannot read or write. Those of us who can, often take these important skills for granted. Indeed if you have grown up reading and writing you have probably forgotten how much effort it takes to learn. You are probably not even aware of how much time you spend reading, it is such a natural, unconscious thing to do.

When people can't read they are excluded from so much human culture.

Literacy and life chances

But the issue of literacy is not just about the less developed nations and whether people are illiterate. In 2002 the OECD revealed, 'Among student characteristics, engagement in reading has the largest median correlation with achievement in reading literacy.' The National Literacy Trust reports, 'Reading for pleasure has been revealed as the most important indicator of the future success of a child. Improvements in literacy at any stage of a person's life can have a profound effect.'

Another report for the National Literacy Trust says 'children and young people who read 50 books or more a year are more likely to enjoy reading and do better at school. And four books a month does seem to be a tipping point.' But it is not just about quantity. Ex-children's laureate Anthony Browne says 'Pleasure, engagement and enjoyment of books is what counts – not simply meeting targets.'

No matter your background, if you want to give yourself the best chance of success in education, develop your interest in reading. If you want to help others, think about how you can support the project of developing literacy around the world. This can start in our own localities. There are people around us who have difficulties in learning, which affect their abilities to communicate and read. People with difficulties related to literacy can feel excluded and vulnerable. The way we treat human beings with additional needs says something about our values.

Success in moving towards Millennium Goals

Hans Rosling points out the danger of 'underestimating the tremendous social change in Asia.' His statistical analysis on health and economic productivity shows life expectancy has grown in less developed countries and family size has shrunk. This is contrary to our stereotypes of developed and developing nations. Rosling says: 'Life expectancy and family size are now almost exactly the same in Vietnam as in the USA . . . This shows Vietnam has caught up. As for poverty, there is much less poverty in Asia than in the 1970s.'

Rosling's talks generate optimism. Improved medicine and social conditions have helped countries to improve prosperity. The Millennium Development Goals Report for 2012 also strikes positive notes, stating:

> **Many countries facing the greatest challenges have made significant progress towards universal primary education**
> Enrolment rates of children of primary school age increased markedly in sub-Saharan Africa, from 58 to 76 per cent between 1999 and 2010. Many countries in that region succeeded in reducing their relatively high out-of-school rates even as their primary school age populations were growing.
>
> **Child survival progress is gaining momentum**
> Despite population growth, the number of under-

five deaths worldwide fell from more than 12.0
million in 1990 to 7.6 million in 2010. And progress
in the less developed world as a whole has
accelerated. Sub-Saharan Africa—the region with
the highest level of under-five mortality—has
doubled its average rate of reduction, from 1.2 per
cent a year over 1990–2000 to 2.4 per cent during
2000–2010.

Millennium Development Goals focused the United
Nations towards actions which prioritise young people.
Countries know their progress in the education and health
of children will be measured and compared with others.

Clearly, there is still much room for further progress. In an
expanded human population, it will be a challenge to ensure
inequality does not become even more of a global threat –
with crippling poverty and hunger destabilising countries.

As the gap between rich and poor grows, it is likely to fuel
a greater sense of injustice.

Some questions for us might be:

1 What steps can be taken internationally to ensure
   Millennium Development Goals are reached?
2 How can we ensure poverty and hunger are
   addressed as the human population expands?
3 What steps should be taken to reduce global
   inequality?

Conclusion

I began by asking five questions:

- What will it mean to be human in 2100?
- How might human beings live good lives in the future?
- How can we make sure humanity does not destroy itself in the process of evolving from where we are now, to where we might be?
- What kind of learning do we need to do as a species to evolve further and survive?
- And finally, to what extent should we feel optimistic about our future?

They are impossible to answer conclusively because, of course, the future hasn't happened yet. Even guessing is difficult. In a TED talk, Iain Goldin says the future is unpredictable and that people who speculate about it almost always get it wrong. He also says the next century could be our greatest century or our worst.

What we can do is say something about the way forward. It is notable that experts often disagree about the future, adopting positive or negative perspectives, in varying ways and degrees, depending on issues. Sometimes they disagree due to political, economic or religious viewpoints. Sometimes about what the facts might be. It is more difficult when it comes to the future.

One thing that makes prediction difficult is uncertainty about exactly how the human population will develop – and much depends on this. The UN has published trend analysis which projects the human population might reach twelve billion by 2100. Others think it may plateau around eight billion. A world of twelve billion would be vastly different from one of eight billion – and much more problematic.

Either way, population is increasing and with it comes more pressure on resources. There may well be a lot more tension between nations, and groups within nations, because of this. Environmental groups worry about depleting natural resources, like plant and animal species. The UN worries about future shortages of water and food. Meanwhile, there is evidence of waste being generated by the way in which we manage resources, such as food, through industrial process.

If current trends continue, there may be greater tensions around the gap between rich and poor: both the gulf between rich and poor nations, as well as the gulf between rich and poor people within nations. The sense of injustice felt throughout the world because of this, could lead to conflict.

Some people see the growing global population as a positive thing, imagining an increasingly connected global community which can collaborate to solve problems. Hans Rosling charts great developments internationally in life expectancy and health. Peter Diamandis highlights potential new technologies which could solve the problems of having clean drinking water and have a revolutionary effect where they are most needed. And Jürgen Habermas finds hope in the development of the modern era:

> Since the beginning of the modern period,
> expanding markets and communications networks

had an explosive force, with simultaneously individualising and liberating consequences for individual citizens . . . Time and again, a sufficient equilibrium between the market and politics was achieved to ensure that the network of social relations between citizens of a political community was not damaged beyond repair. According to this rhythm, the current phase of financial market-driven globalisation should also be followed by a strengthening of the international community.

But strengthening the international community is more difficult to achieve when nation states act from short term self-interest and wealthy nations engage in actions that may seem positive in the short term, but are ultimately unsustainable. There is also the evidence that wealthy nations advocate free markets, but in fact manage their own interests to maintain economic superiority. Francis Wheen explains how controlling international interests have added to the gap between rich and poor:

Growth isn't everything, of course, but . . . it's all that the authorities who have directed policy for most of the developing world – the International Monetary Fund, the World Bank, the US Treasury department – have promised to deliver. The prescriptions imposed by these authorities have created problems and then exacerbated them. Relative disparities in incomes are far wider than twenty years ago, and even in absolute terms there is little evidence of the trickle down effect . . .
The poorest 10 percent of the world's population 400 million people – lived on 72 cents a day in 1980. Ten years later the figure was 79 cents, and by 1999 – after two decades of rampant liberalisation – it had slipped back to 78 cents. In seventy countries people were on average poorer

than they were in 1980. The income of the wretched of the earth hadn't even kept pace with inflation.

Jean-François Rischard argues we need to change the way in which we govern global development and manage change:

The complexity of many global issues and their lack of boundaries don't sit so well with the territorial and hierarchical institutions that are supposed to solve them: the nation states. Nation states know this, and historically their reaction has been to try to respond through treaties and conventions. But they have moved beyond this and created three more contraptions.

To manage global issues we have developed inter-governmental conferences, G20 type groups of countries, global non-governmental organisations (like the WHO and UNICEF). He thinks this is all too cumbersome, slow and unable to affect the change we need. Moreover, nation states are brittle in the face of the global threats. Diseases like AIDs and Ebola do not respect international borders. Financial collapses cut across nations, due to how markets work. And, terrorism weakens the security and identity of countries – as Iraq shows.

He suggests a system of networked governance for issues like poverty allow Global Issues Networks to marshal solutions across nations. He thinks this would allow longer term, global thinking to shape the world's systems. But, it is not how things work at the moment.

Wheen, Habermas and Rischard raise concern about the mechanisms of governance for important global issues. But, the optimism of experts can sometimes depend on their confidence in scientific and technological progress.

Robert Winston's Scientific Manifesto links learning in science to other aspects of citizenship through an inter-disciplinary approach. This allows people (including young people learning about science) to reflect on ethical and social consequences of scientific advance.

But a number of thinkers question how we undertake scientific development to improve human life. On the one side, you have scientific optimists who argue we can invent our way out of future problems – for them challenges are technical. More sceptical thinkers feel there is little hope and we may be embarked on a path towards destruction – current economic and political systems are not equipped to solve the problems we have.

We might ask if the way we organise human affairs right now allows us to see answers we need. Or are we locked into ways of thinking and acting that blind us? Richard Wilkinson and Kate Pickett tell a cautionary tale:

> In 1847, Ignaz Semmelweiss discovered that if doctors washed their hands before attending women in childbirth, it dramatically reduced deaths from puerperal fever. But before his work could have much benefit, he had to persuade people – principally his medical colleagues – to change their behaviour. His real battle was not his initial discovery but what followed on from it. His views were ridiculed and he was driven eventually to insanity and suicide. Much of the medical profession did not take his views seriously until Louis Pasteur and Joseph Lister had developed the germ theory of disease, which explained why hygiene was important.

The Semmelweis story is a good analogy for current challenges in tackling CO_2 emissions and ozone depletion; or inequality; or the issue of lessening resource. We have perhaps heard the message, but either don't believe it or are just not prepared to change the way we are doing things. As seventeenth century philosopher Thomas Hobbes wrote in Leviathan, 'Hell is a truth seen too late.'

Technological developments have the potential to enhance life, but there is also a danger people could become more connected, but also more isolated. The drive for efficiency can rupture the relationships between people and organisations they depend on.

The sense of economic injustice is ironically encouraged by a consumer society, where people are encouraged to identify success with material possession. Tim Kasser says we should, 'Think of materialism as being about three main things: money and what it can buy, appearance and image and fame, popularity, status and power. What holds these values together is the idea of how we appear through the eyes of others.'

Consumerism is programmed to ensure people want more. But in future there will be less. And it will be owned by a smaller proportion of the global population. Some people think things are coming to a head.

For Jules Pretty, consumerism has environmental consequences:

> The consumer culture transformed the old
> assumptions about people and land. Global
> connectedness now illuminates the upsides of
> consumption, and aspirations are converging. But

now come considerable environmental and social
side-effects, so serious they threaten this finite
planet's capacity to resource all our wants.
Conventional economic growth encourages a race
to the top of consumption, even though large
numbers of people currently have no prospect of
escaping poverty or hunger. We still call this progress.

Making best use of the planet's resources is a logistical and
ethical challenge. Pressure on resources is not just about our
views on science, but also our commitment to longer term
sustainability; not just about political views about what we
need to do, but also about the ideas that shape these views;
not just about trade and consumption, but about equity and
poverty. Ultimately, it is about who we are.

Phil Hanlon says we need to think about the world we are
creating:

We all pretty much know how to look after
ourselves. But we often lack the care, the concern
for ourselves to put that knowledge into action. At
the same time that compassion needs to extend to
the whole eco-system and indeed to every person
on earth. In other words, we need a global
consciousness of compassion to be imbued with
the sense of optimism... At the same time we need
courage to... create the societal policies that will
make us more sustainable, healthier and more
equitable.

Future focused education

One thing that could be done relates to education: schools
could do more to enable young people to shape responses
to future issues. But schools are measured by other standards

which do not necessarily equate to challenges young people will encounter in their lives. Andreas Schleicher's *Case for 21st Century Learning* sets the challenge:

> We live in a fast-changing world, and producing more of the same knowledge and skills will not suffice to address the challenges of the future. A generation ago, teachers could expect that what they taught would last their students a lifetime... Conventionally, our approach to problems was to break them down into manageable bits and pieces, confined to narrow disciplines, and then to teach students the techniques to solve them. Today, however, knowledge advances by synthesizing these disparate bits. It demands open-mindedness, making connections between ideas that previously seemed unrelated and becoming familiar with knowledge in other fields.

Jane McGonigal's comments on gaming show the potential of active and collaborative learning to solve the challenges of the future. John Hunter's Peace Game is similar, providing a context, where young people undertake important negotiating roles and focus on big challenges.

At the moment, there are variances in how human rights exist across the world. Learning about human rights can help to develop an international perspective and deepen the sense of shared humanity and global identity in the human race. This might help organs of international cooperation become more effective in protecting human rights internationally. The Dalai Lama said something like this in 2008.

Ken Robinson thinks schools discourage the creativity people need:

Creativity is as important in education as literacy
and we should treat it with the same status . . . All
children have talent and we squander it ruthlessly
. . . By the time most kids become adults, they have
become frightened of being wrong and we run our
companies like this. We stigmatise mistakes. And we
are now running national education systems where
mistakes are the worst things you can make . . . We
are educating people out of their creative capacities.

So, we should focus on rights and global awareness; on
interdisciplinary learning; on creativity and scientific literacy,
as well as ensuring the population is literate and numerate.
And teachers should be supported to do this.

In his career Professor David Hicks developed a body of
work devoted to a future based curriculum. A joint article
with Cathie Holden argues that skills and knowledge of
teachers need to be developed to create a relevant
curriculum for the twenty-first century:

It is vital that ITET [Initial Teacher Education and
Training] programmes find ways of broadening
their remit. There needs to be time and provision
for students to learn strategies for teaching about
global and controversial issues, time for them to
improve their own knowledge and understanding,
and time for them to learn how to critically evaluate
sources of information . . . The world of the early
twenty-first century is complex and fast changing.
Local and national issues, events and trends can
only be understood if set in the wider global
context . . . effective delivery in schools will largely
depend on the understanding, ability and
motivation of student teachers to help young
people make such 'global connections'.

Their research showed the gaps in understanding of global issues that training teachers felt they had and suggests teacher training programmes should address this. The same article refers to a body of other research that shows the extent to which young people feel education about global issues is important:

> One useful source of information relating to young people's global concerns comes from research into their hopes and fears for the future. A study of primary aged children in the UK by Hicks and Holden (1995) showed that their main global concerns related to issues of: war and peace, pollution of the environment, food and poverty, and relationships between countries.

The research confirms that young people worry about the future. The education system needs to speak to them. Teachers need to build a relevant curriculum to address this need in a language that helps them.

If you are sixteen in 2014, you will retire around 2065 (if people are still able to). The year 2100 will be in reach. Some people that age will live to see it. The future is unpredictable. We cannot be sure what will happen. And, we may be embarked on a path that could wipe the species out by then. But, there is hope in global wonders; in the ingenuity of our technological accomplishments; in the shared effort to support Millennium Development Goals; and in the things that bring us together.

We are at an important moment in time. Significant environmental, economic and societal pressures are looming. We may have to live with less. So, we need a narrative of what it means to be a global citizen that relates to everyday life. One that brings peoples together, understanding that injustice could cause greater division, which could in turn lead to destruction.

We need to think deeply about the people we are and want to be. About the future we are building. And how far we feel responsible for future generations. This will come down to how we treat each other. It will also come down to the value we place on justice, equity and health for people around the world who have different racial characteristics, religions and ideas to us. People we may have never met, or may never actually meet. But, who are potentially our friends.

Philosopher Bertrand Russell, speaking at a Nobel Lecture in 1950, expressed concern humanity may not be able to meet future challenges:

> I do not deny that there are better things than selfishness, and that some people achieve these things. I maintain, however, on the one hand, that there are few occasions upon which large bodies of men, such as politics is concerned with, can rise above selfishness, while, on the other hand, there are a very great many circumstances in which populations will fall below selfishness, if selfishness is interpreted as enlightened self-interest.

In the final novel of the late Iain Banks, a character Hol suggests a way of looking at progress:

> . . . there's just the usual slow but eventually steady progress of human morality and behaviour, built up over millennia;... just the spreading of literacy, education and an understanding of how things really work, through research and the dissemination of results of that research through honest media . . .

Everything – print, radio, television, computers, digitalisation, the internet – makes a difference, but nothing makes all of the difference. We build better lives and better worlds slowly, painstakingly, and there are no short cuts, just lots of improvements, most small, a few greater, none decisive.

Final Note

Dear Daughter

I began by saying this book was an act of hope. I end it by stating a challenge for all of us to think more clearly and engage more fully with the problems faced by the world we all inhabit.

There are reasons to be optimistic about future human survival. But also reasons to be concerned about the world we are creating for generations who will follow us. There will be more of us and less resource. And there are some major risks to negotiate. Human life in future may be unrecognisable compared to today.

Citizenship comes down to how we treat each other and in future (in our socio-economic relations) our sense of shared humanity will be tested. We are more connected and closer together than ever. But the history of humanity shows how divisions between peoples can easily arise and become sources of tension. Celebrating cultural and national identities and differences between peoples is important. But, we should remember the basic humanity that binds us and respect the important rights people are entitled to. It is this latter idea that has the potential to ensure a positive future.

We need to practice compassion for the great numbers of people in the world who suffer poverty and violence. The poor are in all countries and suffering is everywhere. That compassion starts with understanding the world and its vastness. It grows through learning about others and fostering interest in exploring the nature of human existence.

Global challenges ahead are complex. Solutions involve developing shared understanding of these problems and an international commitment to addressing them.

And we probably need to change a lot of things we currently do.

We are explorers. Inventors. And, with progress, we are becoming peace builders. We have the capacity to be compassionate in response to global issues. And, at our best, we are capable of great courage and dignity.

But we need to show more care for the children of the world: both those living now; and those still to be born. We need to show regard for the lives these children these children will lead and to create conditions in which they can flourish.

This is the great gift people today can give those who will follow.

Lots of love
Dad

Afterword

Dr Alan Britton

I first met Derek Brown a decade ago; almost immediately it was clear that he had a restless curiosity about the nature of education and about the wider world it inhabits. He had become worried that school students could be academically successful, but still lack resilience, autonomy, and a clear values framework needed to interrogate the world they inhabited.

This first meeting took place against a backdrop of impending curricular change in Scottish education. The system was grappling with a reassertion of the fundamental purposes of schooling, and a reassertion of the values underpinning the entire enterprise of education. This was expressed in a more interdisciplinary view of knowledge as a means to address the complex problems of the twenty-first century, and a globalised context. Derek and his colleagues seized on this rationale and, rather than waiting until the picture became clearer around assessment and qualifications (around a decade later), they forged ahead with educational initiatives that exemplified this approach.

Their willingness to take the lead also resonated with my own pedagogical commitment to a stronger futures orientation to teaching and learning; one that sought to combine elements of science, culture, politics, speculative philosophy and ethical dilemmas in order to rethink and reframe the future. This strand in their teaching actually had a noble, albeit marginalised, genealogy in educational thought, with a small band of advocates such as Fitch and Svengalis, Hicks, and Inayatullah, who have argued that the futures dimension remains largely absent from the curriculum. Even the OECD noted in 2001 that: '. . . forward thinking of this kind has been relatively little developed in education compared with other policy sectors, despite education's fundamental characteristic of yielding benefits over very long time spans.'

Some professions are more easily attuned to long term thinking than others; it is in the lifeblood of actuarial calculations and geologists and economists (at least in theory) are educated to think in the long run. Public health professionals convey preventative messages that emphasise long term consequences of certain patterns of consumption or activity. Yet too often in education such perspectives are absent. As someone engaged in the education of the next generation of teachers I can testify that it is at best touched upon only very briefly in their preparation although there are tentative signs in a number of countries that a new emphasis on *learning for sustainability* might have the potential to promote a greater focus on educational futures.

As this book demonstrates, Derek's goal is entirely consistent with this way of thinking about education: he wishes to encourage young people (and their teachers and parents) to pause for thought about the future, in the face of a contemporary culture in which our attention spans are eroded by ephemeral stimuli and short term gratification. He seeks to provoke a sense of both wonder and anger among his readers. He wants to equip young people with an understanding that recognises both the challenges and opportunities that lie ahead of them individually and as members of a global society, and to make the right choices for themselves and others. Along the way Derek deals unflinchingly with both the light and the dark in humanity, and paints a picture that at times might appear rather pessimistic. However it is notable that he concludes on a note of cautious optimism, grounded in an enlightened sceptical humanism.

Derek has framed this book as a message to his daughter. As a father of two young children I also sometimes reflect on the kind of world we will bequeath to future generations. However this book is much more than a personal note to one individual: it is a manifesto for a more meaningful and purposeful conception of education itself. It is a vision for the future that we ignore at our peril.

Dr Alan Britton, Director of the Education for Global Citizenship Unit at the University of Glasgow

Bibliography

Booklist

Nafeez Ahmed, *A User's Guide to Civilisation and How to Save it*, Pluto Press, London, 2010.

Iain Banks, *The Quarry*, Little Brown, 2013.

Carol Craig, *The Great Takeover*, Argyll Publishing, 2012.

Paul Davies, *The Goldilocks Enigma: Why is the Universe Just Right for Life*, Mariner, 2007.

Karen E. Dill, *How Fantasy Becomes Reality*, Oxford University Press, 2009.

Danny Dorling, *Inequality and the 1%*, Verso, 2014.

Steven Emmott, *Ten Billion*, Penguin 2013.

Jürgen Habermas, *The Theory of Communicative Action*, Volume II, Beacon Press, 1987.

Phil Hanlon and Sandra Carlisle, *After Now: What We Need for a Healthy Scotland*, Argyll Publishing, 2012.

Cathie Holden and David Hicks, 'Making Global Connections: The Knowledge, Understanding and Motivation of Trainee Teachers', *Teaching and Teacher Education, 23(3): 13–23.*

Immanuel Kant, *Perpetual Peace.*

Pentti Lintkova, *Can Life Prevail?*, Arktos, 2009.

Nelson Mandela, *Long Walk to Freedom*, Little Brown and Co. 1995.

Hugh McDiarmid, *'Scotland Small?', Complete Poems,* Volume II, Carcenet, 1994.

Jules Pretty, *The Edge of Extinction, Travels With Enduring People in Vanishing Lands*, Comstock Publishing, 2014.

Jean-Francois Rischard, *High Noon: Twenty Global Problems, Twenty Years to Solve Them*, Basic Books, 2002.

Maurice Roche, *Mega Events and Modernity*, Routledge, 2000.

Bertrand Russell, *History of Western Philosophy*, Routlege, 1984.

Mike Small, *Scotland's Local Food Revolution*, Argyll Publishing, 2013.

Kenneth White, *On Scottish Ground*, Polygon, 1998.

Gore Vidal, *Thomas Love Peacock: The Novel of Ideas*, Abacus, 1993.

R. Wallace and O. Martin-Ortega, *International Law*, Sweet and Maxwell, 2013.

Francis Wheen, *How Mumbo Jumbo Conquered the World*, Harper Perennial, 2004.

Richard Wilkinson and Kate Pickett, *The Spirit Level, Why Equality is Better for Everyone*, Penguin, 2010

Robert Winston, *Bad Ideas?: An arresting history of our inventions*, Bantam Press, 2010

Reports

The Costs of Attaining the Millennium Development Goals, Report, The World Bank.

Third IPPC Report, *Summary for Policy Makers*, 2001.

Joshua M Wiener and Jane Tilly, *Population Aging in the USA: Implications for Public Programmes*, International Journal of Epidemiology, 2002.

Reading for Change, Performance Engagement Across Countries, OECD, 2002.

The Ethics of Human Cloning, UNESCO, 2004.

Gita Sen and Piroska Ostlin, Unequal, Unfair, Ineffective and Inefficient Gender Inequity in Health: Why It Exists And How We Can Change It, Report to the WHO Commission, 2007.

George Dugdale and Christina Clark, *Literacy Changes Lives: An Advocacy Resource*, National Literacy Trust, 2008.

D. Gentile, *Pathological Video Game Use Among Youth Ages 8 to 18: A National Study,* National Centre for Biotechnology Information (USA), June 2009.

Global Inequality: Beyond the Bottom Billion, UNICEF, 2011.

Christina Clark and Lizzie Poulton, *Is Four the Magic Number*, National Literacy Trust, 2011.

United Nations Department of Economic and Social Affairs, *Probabilistic Population Projections* (2012 Revision).

Gender Inequality in Education, Employment and Entrepreneurship, Final Report to the MCM, OECD, 2012

The *Uganda AIDS Commission Report* is available through the UN AIDS Organisation, 2012.

Joshua M Wiener and Jane Tilly, *Population Aging in the USA: Implications for Public Programmes*, International Journal of Epidemiology, 2002.

Thrive At Five: Comparative Child Development At School-Entry Stage, Save the Children, 2012.

Fifth IPPC Report, *Summary for Policy Makers*, 2013.

UN Report on *Millennium Development Goals*, 2013.

Nick Bostrom, *Existential Risk Prevention as a Global Priority*, Faculty of Philosophy & Oxford Martin School, University of Oxford, 2013.

Report on the Alleged Use of Chemical Weapons in the Ghouta Area of Damascus on 21 August 2013, United Nations Mission Report. 2013.

Diarrhoeal Disease, *World Health Organisation*, 2013.

Joseph Hilgard, Christopher R. Englehardt, and Bruce D. Batholow, *Individiual differences in Motives, Preferences and Patholbogy, in Video Games, the Gaming Attitudes, Motives and Experiences Scales*, Frontiers in Psychology, September 2013.

Ian Goldin and Pascal Lamy, *Overcoming Short-Termism, A Pathway for Global Progress*, The Washington Quarterly, 2014.

The Kingdom of Swaziland UNAIDS report, 2014.

The United Nations *International Telecommunications Union* report (2014).

House of Commons *Report for MPs on Common Fisheries Policy*, 2014.

Global Wealth Report 2014, Credit Suisse, 2014.

Report of the Special Rapporteur on extrajudicial, summary or arbitrary executions, United Nations, September 2013.

Literacy Changes Lives, National Literacy Trust, 2014.

Book Series from Argyll Publishing and the Centre for Confidence and Well-being

This series of short books is designed to stimulate and communicate new thinking and ways of living. The first volumes appeared in late 2012 priced from £5.99.

Series editor and advisory group: Carol Craig of the Centre for Confidence and Well-being is the series editor. She is supported by a small advisory group comprising Fred Shedden, Chair of the Centre's Board, Professor Phil Hanlon and Jean Urquhart MSP.

Title: **Scotland's Local Food Revolution**
Author: Mike Small
ISBN: 978 1 908931 26 9

Title: **After Now – What next for a healthy Scotland?**
Authors: Phil Hanlon and Sandra Carlisle
ISBN: 978 1 908931 05 4

Title: **The Great Takeover – How materialism, the media and markets now dominate our lives**
Author: Carol Craig
ISBN: 978 1 908931 06 1

Title: **The New Road – Charting Scotland's inspirational communities**
Authors: Alf Young and Ewan Young
ISBN: 978 1 908931 07 8

Title: **Letting Go– Breathing new life into organisations**
Authors: Tony Miller and Gordon Hall
ISBN: 978 1 908931 49 8

Title: **Raising Spirits**
Authors: Jenny Mollison, Judy Wilkinson and Rona Wilkinson
ISBN: 978 1 908931 59 7

Title: **Schooling Scotland**
Authors: Daniel Murphy
ISBN: 978 1 908931 61 0

Also published as **e**-books